Chains of Slavery

Chains of Slavery

The End Began at the Beginning
With an Institution

Brian Ridolfi

RESOURCE *Publications* · Eugene, Oregon

CHAINS OF SLAVERY
The End Began at the Beginning With an Institution

Resource Publications
An Imprint of Wipf and Stock Publishers
199 W. 8th Ave., Suite 3
Eugene, OR 97401

www.wipfandstock.com

PAPERBACK ISBN: 978-1-7252-8862-1
HARDCOVER ISBN: 978-1-7252-8863-8
EBOOK ISBN: 978-1-7252-8864-5

05/12/22

What you are about to read was written
four years before the events of 2020 and 2021.

If you never care to know,
you will never know to care.

Heads are in the sand
before they are in a noose.

Fall asleep complacent
and you will wake up oppressed.

Contents

CHAPTER 1

The Cell

Without freedom of conscience,
freedom is not conscious.

"THAT'S QUITE A SHINER," he said. Expecting a monster, I turned around and saw a benevolent old man instead. "My name is Paul. What's yours?" he asked.

"Tim, short for Timothy," I answered.

"Good to meet you," the man said. We shook hands and sat on our bunks. "So how did you end up here?" he inquired. I explained to him I got in a fight with another prisoner, originally I was incarcerated for theft, work was scarce and so was food, so I stole to survive.

"Sounds unfortunate," he said with a sigh. I was perplexed. How could a guy like this be in here with all this human filth? I couldn't picture him assaulting someone. Homicide! Forget it. Terrorism? To me it looked like he wouldn't harm a fly. I thought *He's here for some other reason, probably something nonviolent*. I asked him, "What was your crime?"

He said, "Proselytizing." I never heard of that. I supposed it was something bad if it landed him in this hell hole.

"Proselytizing," I asked. "What does that mean?"

"I preach the Gospel. I'm a Christian evangelist" he answered. I was told Christians were a fringe group of knuckle dragging political extremists.

I asked him, "Are you saying you were incarcerated for being a Christian?"

"No," he replied. "I'm locked up for proselytizing, not for being a Christian. You can practice Christianity as long as it's the state's accepted form of Christianity. You see it's okay to do anything in America provided the government approves of it. Otherwise, it's a crime against 'Harmony and Tolerance.'"

A light suddenly came on. He was a dissident. The state hated dissidents more than anyone else, even mass murderers. I saw many of them rounded up, carried off, never to be seen again. Now I knew where they were taking them, into isolation. I said, "Crime against the state, it doesn't get more serious than that!"

"Tell me about it," he replied.

• • •

It was eleven years after the Revolution when my conversation with Paul began, Friday, February 28, 2048 to be exact. That was the day I met him in prison and the day my life changed forever. America was cold and dark back then, not unlike my prison cell. There wasn't much to live for in those days. The lights all but faded, and salt lost its savor. Things were so bad, I'd given up hope. Little did I know my perspective would change. Believe it or not, it began with a squabble over drinking utensils.

• • •

That same day at supper I noticed the cups that were usually passed out on the tables in the prison's mess hall every night before dinner were missing. I looked around, but I didn't see them. A gentleman, and I use that term loosely, at another table had them all. I got up and confronted the Cretan. I said did you take the cups.

He responded in kind, or I should say not so kindly, "I didn't take anything." I didn't notice how big he was until he stood on his massive feet. "Do you think you can intimidate me?" he shouted.

Without even thinking I replied, "Oh, I believe I can." That was my first mistake. Next thing I know the beast was on me like a fly on you know what. As I flew across the table, regret came to mind. Before that, I had never realized one human being could throw another so far. Lying there on the floor, I obtained valuable time. I started contemplating my next move.

He made his way back to me and said, "You're a dead man." By then it was clear, I had riled a hornet's nest. The strength of this guy was incredible. I tried fending him off, but he was just too powerful. My punches had no effect on him, nor did anything else I tried. A circle of people quickly formed around us. At this point I was sucking wind and in pain. I thought *If I don't do something soon, I probably won't make it out of this situation alive.* He came at me again, but this time he was laughing fiendishly. "Why don't you just give up?" he scoffed. Believe me, I wanted to, but something told me if I did, he would've killed me.

It was at that point I realized his overconfidence gave me an opportunity. I noticed he stopped paying attention to me and was playing to the crowd. He thought he had already beaten me. He couldn't have been more wrong. Though I was tired and bloodied, I still had some fight left in me.

He knelt right in front of me without so much as a smidgeon of concern for his own safety just to taunt me. "Let me get those cups for you," he said, "so I can shove them up your . . ." He stood, walked toward the crowd and exposed his backside. I didn't waste any time. Once he took his eyes off me, I pounced. At first the behemoth was shocked, but unshaken. He tried reaching around, but that didn't work. Then he tried running backward and slamming me against the wall, but that effort also failed. I held on to his well-muscled neck with every ounce of strength I had. Finally something I did had an effect on him. I felt energy and strength leave his body as I squeezed as hard as I could. He dropped to one knee, then to two. Eventually, he was flat on his face with me on his back. He was out cold. I had cut off the flow of blood to his brain with a jujitsu sleeper hold, a move I had learned on the streets. Thinking back, had I not had to fight to survive outside of prison, more than likely I wouldn't have survived that day in prison.

All the raucous got the attention of the guards. They hurried over and subdued me. That's how I ended up in isolation. And that's where my perspective changed.

• • •

After the fight was over prison administrators put me in the penitentiary's high security wing, or HSW as it was called. It was a place no man wanted to be. Immediately, my eyes were opened. It wasn't like the wing where I had been housed earlier. There I could play cards, participate in the occasional pickup game of basketball, and be free to roam around inside and assemble outside on the yard. In the HSW I had no such liberty.

My new home was drab, sterile, and downright depressing. What little hope I had vanished once I saw the ugliness of that place. The guards were different too. "Cold automatons" is the best way to describe them. No compassion in their deeds, no joy in their hearts. Enmity could be seen behind their flat soulless eyes. The inmates were even scarier. Psychopaths, sociopaths, creatures from horror flicks, you name it, they were there. Despite the horror, the HSW is where Paul and I talked.

• • •

Once I was settled in, Paul asked me a question. "Tim, what do you think is the most serious crime there is?"

I paused for a moment to answer, "Probably murder."

"That's serious, no question about that," he responded. "Think a bit harder. What's worse than violating a person or violating their property?"

"I don't know," I answered.

"Violating their conscience, forcing them to do what they know is evil." I pondered what he said and agreed. He asked, "Where are we?"

"In prison," I responded.

He asked, "What's a prison?"

"A building that holds criminals," I told him.

"It can be," he said. "Be more specific."

"A facility for punishment?" I didn't know what to say.

He replied, "In the absolute sense."

"I have no idea," I answered.

"Tim, a prison is a place of confinement," he cried out. He then asked, "Where were you before you were taken into custody?"

"Free!" I shouted.

"Were you really?" he asked.

"I was freer than I am in here," I argued.

He said, "Are you sure about that? Is it really that much different beyond these penitentiary walls?" He had a point. There was little opportunity on the outside; every day was a struggle just to survive. I lived off government handouts like everyone else. The state doled out provisions. Earning your own scratch was very difficult. If I wanted to eat, I had to do what the politicians wanted.

I said, "You're right, whether inside or outside this jail, government dictates."

"Good Tim," he responded. "I'm glad you see police states are prisons."[1]

"It wasn't always like this," he said. "There was a time when individuals had rights. America was originally a constitutional republic. Let me show you something." He sat up, looked to see if any guards were coming, and shimmied underneath his bunk. "I have some resources you might be interested in." Behind some loose bricks below his bunk were books.

"Where did you get those?" I asked. "I've never seen a printed book before! They were banned years ago."

"Keep quiet, Tim!" he said. "Don't let the guards hear you. The government didn't destroy them all." I was shocked because after the Revolution the army seized all libraries, both public and private, destroyed whatever offensive books it could, confiscated the rest, digitized them, and limited our access to them.

I asked Paul how he had gotten the books inside the HSW of all places. He said, "A guard smuggled them in for me. He was different. He had a conscience. He hated what he saw and wanted to help. I told him, 'Men become history when they fail to learn it.'[2] He concurred. A group of renegades dedicated to preserving knowledge provided the books. They'll remain anonymous. The guard contacted them, acquired the books, slipped them past security, delivered them to me, and, courageously, he paid the ultimate price."

"What do you mean?" I asked.

"He was caught," Paul replied.

I asked, "Is he somewhere in here with us?"

"No Tim," he answered. "He's dead. The prison administration executed him for treason. Like I said, 'He paid the ultimate price.' My dear friend is gone now, but the books remain. The authorities haven't found them. I like to think my brother didn't die in vain."

The look on his face was sobering. You could tell this man had meant a lot to him. They must've been more than just friends; it was almost as if they were family.

• • •

"I have a copy of the original *United States Constitution*," Paul said, "Take a look at this."

> The United States shall guarantee to every State in this Union a Republican Form of Government, and shall protect each of them against Invasion; and on Application of the Legislature, or of the Executive (when the Legislature cannot be convened) against domestic Violence.[3]

"So what's a republican form of government?" I asked.

He said, "It's a government in which supreme power resides in a body of citizens entitled to vote and is exercised by elected officers and representatives responsible to them and governing according to law." Paul again reached beneath his bunk into the secret chamber and removed a book. "Here's another reference I find useful. It's called *Chronicle of America*. Please read this section."

I grasped the colossal book and began to read.

> During the first decades of American independence, national debate centered largely on the nature of the new federal government. Although the founders had envisioned a political system free of political parties, identifiable factions quickly emerged, expressing distinctive views of the nation's future. The Federalists, who looked to Alexander Hamilton for guidance and leadership, envisioned a strong central government dominated by an enlightened elite and promoting economic growth and industrial development. The Republicans, whose patron saint was Thomas Jefferson, favored an agrarian society, states' rights and the supremacy of the "common man." The debate between these two factions (few yet considered them actual "parties") dominated American politics in its first decades and culminated in a bitter presidential campaign between Jefferson and John Adams in 1800. So important did Americans consider the issues in the campaign that Jefferson's victory was widely described as "the revolution of 1800."[4]

He said, "You see, Tim, not only was a republican form of government guaranteed in the Constitution, the people preferred it over federalism early on."

"Funny, I was told America was a democracy before the Revolution," I retorted.

"No Tim," he said. "That isn't true. There has never been a true democracy anywhere in the world. Not even in Greece where the idea was conceived. The Greek empire was governed by a king named Alexander the Great. After he died it was governed by four dynasties, the Antigonid, Seleucid, Ptolemaic, and Attalid dynasties. Democratic rule in an absolute sense is impossible."

I told him, "I don't understand."

He answered, "Democracy simply means government by the people. Tim, can the people make every single political decision?"

"I suppose they can," I answered.

He said, "Really Tim? Did the electorate go to Washington, D.C. to cast their vote every time a decision had to be made?"

"No, of course not," I remarked.

"Why's that?" he asked. "Because there were millions of registered voters. It would've been a logistical nightmare and arduous. That's why they sent representatives. Tim, the United States wasn't a democracy. It was a representative democracy, a republic. More specifically, it was a constitutional republic. The US government was divided into three separate but equal branches, the legislative, the executive, and the judicial branches. It was so to prevent any one branch from acquiring too much power. Checks and balances!"

Paul picked up the original *United States Constitution* and told me to read.

> All legislative Powers herein granted shall be vested in a Congress of the United States, which shall consist of a Senate and House of Representatives.[5]

> The House of Representatives shall be composed of Members chosen every second Year by the People of the several States, and the Electors in each State shall have the Qualifications requisite for Electors of the most numerous Branch of the State Legislature . . .[6]

> The Senate of the United States shall be composed of two Senators from each State, [chosen by the Legislature thereof,] for six Years; and each Senator shall have one Vote . . .[7]

He interrupted me. "Article I Section 3 was amended. Look here."

> The Senate of the United States shall be composed of two Senators from each State, elected by people thereof, for six years; and each Senator shall have one vote. The electors in each State shall have the qualifications requisite for electors of the most numerous branch of the State legislatures . . .[8]

"What do you mean amended?" I asked.

He answered, "The framers allowed the Constitution to be revised. Look here."

> The Congress, whenever two thirds of both Houses shall deem it necessary, shall propose Amendments to this Constitution, or, on the Application of the Legislatures of two thirds of the several States, shall call a Convention for purposing Amendments, which, in either Case, shall be valid to all Intents and Purposes, as Part of

> this Constitution, when ratified by the Legislatures of three fourths
> of the several States, or by Conventions in three fourths thereof, as
> the one or the other Mode of Ratification may be proposed by the
> Congress; . . .[9]

"Keep reading," he said.

> The executive Power shall be vested in a President of the United
> States of America. He shall hold his Office during the Term of four
> Years, and, together with the Vice President, chosen for the same
> Term, . . .[10]

> The judicial Power of the United States, shall be vested in one su-
> preme Court, and in such inferior Courts as the Congress may
> from time to time ordain and establish . . .[11]

"I never heard any of this before!" I exclaimed. "This is all new to me."

"America was a nation of laws," Paul explained. "Representatives elected by the people were sent to Washington, D.C. and to state houses as ministers to do the people's business. What do you think kept legislators and executors from usurping power?"

"The people through democratic elections?" I replied.

"No Tim!" he shouted. "Voters can replace their representatives, they can't stop them from seizing authority. Think for moment. What if every candidate was corrupt? Democracy is insufficient in that case. When both options are bad, the outcome is bad. Democracy does not guarantee autonomy.[12] It is just as easy to choose slavery as it is sovereignty."[13]

"So what kept them from usurping power?" I asked.

"The Constitution is what kept representatives in line," Paul replied. "On August 2, 1788, anti-Federalists proposed a bill of rights be added to the Constitution." He hoisted *Chronicle of America* and told me to read.

> Federalist hopes for unanimous ratification of the Constitution
> faded today as North Carolina refused to approve it. The delegates
> insisted that a second Constitutional Convention be called to draw
> up a bill of rights and consider as series of amendments. Many
> of the delegates voting today are self-sufficient frontiersmen who
> think their rights in such matters as practicing religion and bearing
> arms will be violated by creating a new federal government. One
> anti-Federalist leader, William Goudy, warned that a bill of rights
> was necessary to prevent tyranny. 'We know that private interest
> governs mankind generally,' he said. 'Power belongs originally to

the people, but if rulers be not well guarded, that power may be usurped from them.'[14]

"The *Bill of Rights* was proposed on September 25, 1789, and was ratified effective December 15, 1791. The first ten constitutional amendments made up the *Bill of Rights*, which guaranteed such liberties as freedom of religion, speech, and the press, freedom to assemble and to keep and bear arms, and the right to due process. The *Bill of Rights* assured every American the rights 'endowed by their Creator,'[15] weren't trampled upon.

"In the end they're really only two choices, the rule of law, or the rule of men. Tyranny is tyranny. To those under oppression, the number of despots is neither here nor there.[16] Tyranny of the mob and a mob of tyranny both mob the citizenry.[17] The *Bill of Rights* protected individuals from governmental tyranny, and from the majority."

I said, "I see what you're saying. What changed all that?"

"The end began at the beginning with an institution," Paul replied.

CHAPTER 2

The Institution

Slavery is demanded whenever a demand
for slaves is created.

I ASKED PAUL WHAT institution he was referring to. He said, "Early Americans called it 'the peculiar institution.'"

"The peculiar institution?" I reacted.

"Slavery," he replied.

I told him, "Slavery has been illegal for some time."

"You're right," he answered. "The institution of slavery has been illegal in America since 1865. The story doesn't end there." I asked him what he meant. He said, "The consequences of slavery are still haunting us, even today. Slavery started a chain of events that caused America to go full circle. Slavery for one group of people produced slavery for all people."

I told him, "Now you're speaking gibberish."

He said, "Am I? In order to understand what I'm saying, I must start at the beginning. The Spanish began trading slaves to the New World in 1517. Look here."

> Seeking to quiet Dominican protests over Indian slavery, King Carlos I has granted an 'asiento de Negros,' the first European monopoly for the importation of African slaves to the Indies.[18]

"That was centuries ago!" I yelled. "What does any of this have to do with where we are now?"

Annoyed Paul answered, "Please let me continue. The first slaves arrived at the colony in Jamestown, August 20, 1619. Read, Tim."

'There came in a Dutch man-of-warre that sold us 20 negars,' reports settler John Rolfe. Welcomed by the English colonists as a useful addition to the labor force, these Africans, the first to be brought to the settlement, are indentured servants who will be free after a term of service. Most indentured servants, in return for their passage to America, have agreed to serve for a period of five years. When that time is completed, they may buy land and, in general, act as full citizens of Jamestown, although many end up being tenant farmers, working fields along the James River. It is not known whether the African immigrants have freely consented to these terms.[19]

"Indentured servitude was the first step toward slavery. What we see today began innocently enough with debtors. The first Africans brought to the colonies were bondservants, not slaves. Nobody owned them. They were free to go once their debt was fulfilled, and race didn't matter. In those days a white man could be a bondservant just the same as a black man. In fact, a white man could be the bondservant of a black man."

I said, "How did debtors living in the 17th century bring America down in the 21st century?"

He said, "Bond servitude remained in place for decades until about the mid-1600s." Then he hoisted *Chronicle of America* over to me once again and told me to read.

The profitable but unpleasant trade of slaving has become an American industry with ships now frequently leaving Boston harbor for raids along the West African coast. There, natives are captured or purchased by the Americans and taken to Barbados, where they are traded for salt, tobacco, sugar and wine. These valuable commodities are sold in Boston at a huge profit. In fact, the profits have been so great as to encourage the continuance and growth of this trade in North American ports. The market in Barbados ships slaves to colonies throughout the Americas.[20]

"Here's where everything changed forever. In 1645 Africans were being kidnapped from their homeland and taken to the New World for no reason other than their skin color. Slavery took off because human trafficking was lucrative. Initially, black Africans were indentured servants, but they ended up a commodity when slave trading became profitable."

I said to Paul, "I follow, but none of this explains why America is a prison."

"You've been a good sport, Tim," he said, "so I'll cut to the chase. It's cause and effect."

"Please go on," I said.

"Something ordinary like bond servitude can develop into something terrible, such as slavery," he remarked. "It has the ability to taint everything downstream. Though slavery may be dead in America, its affects aren't. Though slavery may've had an innocuous start, its end was horrific. Let me explain. Bond servitude was the beginning of slavery, and slavery was the beginning of much more."

I said, "Now you've got my attention. Tell me more."

• • •

"Slavery was officially institutionalized March 13, 1660 in Virginia," he said, "with a statute limiting tax on the sale of slaves.[21] By the middle of the 17th century blacks were considered servants for life. Most white bondservants moved on with their lives, becoming productive citizens once their period of indenture was complete. The thousands of black bondservants remaining in Virginia were seldom afforded the same treatment. Laws kept them under bondage."

I said to him, "I don't understand why black bondservants were treated different from white ones."

He answered, "I told you before, 'Human trafficking was lucrative.'" Paul looked outside the cell to see if any guards were standing there, then he put his ear to the door to hear if anyone was approaching. "I guess the coast is clear," he said. Then he reached into his secret chamber.

I said, "Wow! Is that what I think it is?"

He answered, "It's a *Bible*. Yes."

I told him, "You know you can get in serious trouble just for having one of those."

"You think I'm not aware of that?" he replied. "Many of my friends are dead because they tried to distribute them."

I said, "A teacher of mine told me the *Bible* is full of seditious material."

He responded, "Not unless you think truth is seditious." I'll never forget his next words. "Sound wisdom sounds odd in a world deaf to God.[22] Conventional wisdom becomes unconventional if conventions change.[23] Common sense is uncommon among the commonly corrupted.[24]

"Back to your question about 'why black bondservants were treated different from white ones.' People got rich off the slave trade. At the heart of slavery was the love of money. Read this."

> And having food and raiment let us be therewith content. But they that will be rich fall into temptation and a snare, and into many foolish and hurtful lusts, which drown men in destruction and perdition. For the love of money is the root of all evil: which while some coveted after, they have erred from the faith, and pierced themselves through with many sorrows. (1 Timothy 6:8–10 *KJV*)

I told Paul, "I heard that saying before, only I heard it said that 'money is the root of all evil.'"

He said, "Read it carefully. The love of money is evil, not money itself. Many people misrepresent the Scriptures. Money results from labor, and labor is good because it produces fruit. We all need fruit to survive. Right? We exchange money for goods and services we need instead of labor and wares, because swapping currency is easier than bartering. Simply said, money is a device used to acquire things. Money is amoral. It's a necessity, like air."

I said, "Yes, but rich people have it all, the rest of us are left with nothing."

"I'm glad you said that," Paul reacted, "because therein lies the problem. It's when we can never have enough money. Avarice is the sin."

I asked, "What's avarice?"

He said, "It's an unquenchable desire for wealth or gain. It's what causes people to do anything, even evil, for more money and power. You see, Tim, avarice is never satisfied.[25] Desire always reaches higher.[26] An insatiable beast never has enough upon which to feast.[27] The *Bible* says it best."

> Moreover the profit of the earth is for all: the king himself is served by the field. He that loveth silver shall not be satisfied with silver; nor he that loveth abundance with increase: this is also vanity. (Ecclesiastes 5:9–10 *KJV*)

"The thing that's evil isn't money, it's the human heart. Read."

> The heart is deceitful above all things, and desperately wicked: who can know it? (Jeremiah 17:9 *KJV*)

"Tim, evil dwells in men. Men do not dwell in evil.[28] Nothing is inherently evil. Evil becomes evil when it rebels against God.[29] Money doesn't corrupt because it's external. It may tempt, but it won't tarnish. Jesus Christ said it this way:"

> . . . Are ye also yet without understanding? Do not ye yet understand, that whatsoever entereth in at the mouth goeth into the belly, and is cast out into the draught? But those things which proceed out of the mouth come forth from the heart; and they defile the man. For out of the heart proceed evil thoughts, murders, adulteries, fornications, thefts, false witness, blasphemies: These are the things which defile a man: but to eat with unwashen hands defileth not a man. (Matthew 15:16–20 *KJV*)

"Blacks were treated differently because they were exploitable. Slave traders wanted to line their own pockets. It's safe to say those involved in the slave trade knew it was wrong, but they didn't care. As long as their wealth increased, their morals decreased. Their desire for money trumped their demand for justice. Freedom from within left blacks without freedom. The limitless quest for more left the fledgling nation with fewer limits."

"Hold on!" I shouted. "You're going too fast! Tell me plainly!"

Paul said, "Cupidity lead to stupidity. Slavery didn't just affect slaves, it split freemen as well. Few colonists owned slaves, but slavery divided all colonists."

• • •

"Not everyone supported slavery. Many didn't," he said. "Some tried to end the institution. In 1769 Thomas Jefferson before becoming president took a major step. Look."

> Recently elected to the House of Burgesses, scientist and free-thinker Thomas Jefferson has, in his first legislative effort, introduced a measure calling for the emancipation of the slaves.[30]

"Four years later in 1774 George Washington, before he became president, did the same in signing the *Fairfax Resolves*."

> George Washington today signed the Fairfax Resolves, which bar the importation of slaves and threaten to put a halt to all colonial exports to England. The influential landowner George Mason is the author of the document, which pledges America's loyalty to Britain. But the resolutions stipulate that exports are to end within the month unless the King faces up to the grievances of

the colonists. Washington, although he owns slaves, agreed to the sections that call for an end to the 'wicked, cruel and unnatural trade.'[31]

"On April 9, 1776 in Philadelphia, shortly before the *Declaration of Independence* was issued to King George the 3rd of England, the Continental Congress called for an end to the slave trade.[32] It did not avail. Unfortunately, colonial efforts to end slavery came short, and the institution remained. America gained independence from England in 1783 after a bloody revolutionary war that lasted six and a half years. The triumphant former colonists held a convention four years later in 1787 in Philadelphia to draft a constitution. The issue of slavery was brought up then. Though it was contested, Southern interests ultimately won out. Read, Tim."

> The Southerners did manage to prevail in one of the most emotional debates of the session, the argument over the abolition of slavery. Many delegates consider the practice hideous, but the convention delayed a move to outlaw it. George Mason of Virginia broke ranks with his fellow Southerners when he argued, 'The poor despise labor when performed by slaves . . . Every master of slaves is born a petty tyrant. They bring the judgment of heaven upon a country.'[33]

"The *Constitutional Convention* in Philadelphia fell short. Slavery was vital to the Southern economy. Elsewhere in the world around the same time the slave trade was being eliminated. On March 25, 1807, in England, the British Parliament ended the slave trade.[34] The same year in March, Thomas Jefferson, as president, once again tried to do the same."

> At the insistence of President Jefferson, Congress has passed a law that prohibits the importation of slaves from Africa, effective next January 1.[35]

"Although Congress passed a law in 1807 banning the slave trade, it was widely ignored.[36] By the mid-19th century America remained the only Anglo-Saxon state still permitting slavery. On August 1, 1834, slavery was abolished throughout the British Empire."[37]

• • •

I said, "Why wasn't slavery abolished in the US as it was in England?"

Paul answered, "That's a good question. It's hard to say exactly why . . . because of economics certainly, also for religious reasons."

I said, "I don't understand."

He said, "There's a religion that justifies slavery."

I jumped in, "You mean the *Old Testament*? It validates slavery I've been told."

"No, Tim, that isn't true," he reacted. "The *Bible* doesn't justify slavery. In fact, it condemns it. Let me show you."

> And he that stealeth a man, and selleth him, or if he be found in his hand, he shall surely be put to death. (Exodus 21:16 *KJV*)

> If a man be found stealing any of his brethren of the children of Israel, and maketh merchandise of him, or selleth him; then that thief shall die; and thou shalt put evil away from among you. (Deuteronomy 24:7 *KJV*)

"Slave traders were kidnapping and selling Africans for profit; according to Old Testament law, they should've been executed. That's a far cry from justification. Capturing noncombatants for monetary gain against their will is a capital offense by Old Testament standards."

I said to Paul, "Okay, if it's not Judaism and Christianity, then what religion are you talking about?"

"Evolution," he replied.

I said, "That isn't a religion. That's science."

"Is it really?" he challenged. Then he asked, "What's science?"

I told him, "Science is truth."

To which he responded, "How do you know that's true?"

"Because what's true is science!" I explained to him.

Paul started laughing. "That's called a tautology. Science is truth because what's true is science, and what's true is science because science is truth. Tim, that's called circular reasoning." I saw his point. He told me, "Science is a method for determining causes. Modern science is really scientism. By its nature it's naturalism.[38]

"Science was a method for questioning. Now, it's a dogma not to be questioned."[39] I asked him what's the difference between science and scientism.

He said, "Science simply means 'the state of knowing.' Scientism on the other hand is 'an exaggerated trust in the efficacy of the methods of natural science.' You see, Tim, scientists look for causes everywhere, and naturalists only look for them in the natural.[40] Not all scientists are naturalists, and no naturalist is a true scientist. Naturalism limits science. It's predicated on a principle."

"What principle is that?" I asked.

"That all causes are natural causes and that supernatural causes aren't scientific." he answered. "The statement you made, 'Evolution isn't religion, it's science' is a great example. Presupposed ideals produce presupposed ideas.[41] Bargains not sought are never bought, and ideas which go uninspected go undetected.[42] Tim, never throw out any hypothesis without testing it first. If you rule out any possibility, you might as well rule out every possibility."[43]

Paul was right. What did I know about science? I just assumed evolution was true because scientists said it was. It suddenly dawned on me; *I was excluding God, not because of lack of evidence, instead, because He's supernatural.*

I said, "I smell what you're cooking, but hasn't 'separation of church and state' always been the law of the land?"

He smirked. "It wasn't! If it was," he said, "then the United States government is violating its own law! Naturalism is in every sense a religion, and it's endorsed by the United States government. Just because scientists say naturalism is irreligious, it doesn't mean it isn't a religious claim. Naturalism by its nature is religious. Tim, neutral governments don't exist. Strict secular governments are nothing more than 'atheocracies.'[44] Besides, you won't find the words 'separation of church and state' in the original constitution, or in any other founding document for that matter. You'll find them in a letter Thomas Jefferson wrote to a committee of Baptists in Danbury, Connecticut. In the letter he said:"

> . . . Believing with you that religion is a matter which lies solely between Man & his God, that he owes account to none other for his faith or his worship, that the legitimate powers of government reach actions only, & not opinions, I contemplate with sovereign reverence that act of the whole American people which declared that their legislature should 'make no law respecting an establishment of religion, or prohibiting the free exercise thereof,' thus building a wall of separation between Church & State . . .[45]

"This is what he was saying: he intended to uphold the first amendment to the *United States Constitution* in accordance with the will of the American people, and to keep government out of their church. Thus, he was pledging his support for freedom of worship. The words 'make no law respecting an establishment of religion, or prohibiting the free exercise thereof' were written in the original constitution,[46] but the words 'thus building a wall of separation between Church & State' weren't. Critics of religion, particularly Christianity, love *The Establishment Clause*, and they should, because it puts a limit on government. But they ignore the all-important phrase 'or prohibiting the free exercise thereof.' They like the fact government can't establish a religion, but they don't accept the idea government didn't always limit religious expression either. The clause went both ways. You see, Tim, the 'wall of separation between Church & State' Thomas Jefferson spoke of, kept the state from the church, not the church from the state."

• • •

"You say evolution is a religion," I remarked. "How so?"

"Because it's built upon faith," Paul answered.

I said, "Come on. Evolution is a scientific fact. Faith is reserved for backward thinking superstitious Neanderthals, not for rational people. That statement is ridiculous."

"Is it really?" he retorted. "Tell me, Tim, what do know about evolution?" Reluctant to answer, I resorted to what my teachers said.

"What about the fossil record?"

Paul laughed. "It's a record against evolution. Have you ever heard of the *Cambrian Explosion*?"

"No," I answered.

"Let me enlighten you," he said. "The *Cambrian Explosion* explodes the *Theory of Evolution*.[47] According to evolutionary theory, all organisms on earth evolved from a universal ancestor 3.8 billion years ago. That's not what we see in the fossil record. We see an abrupt appearance of nearly all major known animal groups (phylums) in full form in Cambrian strata. Darwin himself knew the fossil record presented a substantial challenge to his theory. He wrote:"

> Why then is not every geological formation and every stratum full of such intermediate links? Geology assuredly does not reveal any such finely graduated organic chain, and this, perhaps, is the most obvious and gravest objection which can be argued against my theory.[48]

"Tim, if the fossil record shows stasis, Darwin's theory has no basis."
He asked, "What else you got?"

Again I drew from my formal education.

"What about missing links?"

"What about them? They're missing," he scoffed.

"That's not true. Archaeopteryx is a link between dinosaurs and birds,"
I argued.

"Are you sure?" he countered. "Back in 1861 when it was discovered in
Germany most scientists believed it was a bird. However, fast-forward 150
years later, Chinese scientists Xing Xu, Hailu You, Kai Du, and Fenglu Han
reclassified Archaeopteryx in 2011. Read this journal."

> Archaeopteryx is widely accepted as being the most basal bird,
> and accordingly it is regarded as central to understanding avia-
> lan origins; however, recent discoveries of derived maniraptorans
> have weakened the avialan status of Archaeopteryx. Here we re-
> port a new Archaeopteryx-like theropod from China. This find
> further demonstrates that many features formerly regarded as
> being diagnostic of Avialae, including long and robust forelimbs,
> actually characterize the more inclusive group Paraves (composed
> of the avialans and the deinonychosaurs). Notably, adding the new
> taxon into a comprehensive phylogenetic analysis shifts Archae-
> opteryx to the Deinonychosauria. Despite only tentative statistical
> support, this result challenges the centrality of Archaeopteryx in
> the transition to birds. If this new phylogenetic hypothesis can be
> confirmed by further investigation, current assumptions regard-
> ing the avialan ancestral condition will need to be re-evaluated.[49]

"Archaeopteryx isn't a transitional form to anything, like all other
known fossils."

I gave it one last shot.

"All right, Paul, I have a scientific fact you can't deny. The earth is more
than six thousand years old."

He asked, "How do you know that?" I felt I had him against the ropes
this time.

I said smugly, "Because scientists can date the rocks with radiometric
dating." Unbeknownst to me, he had a reasonable response for this assertion as well.

"Radiometric dating is wholly based on the assumption of uniformitarianism." He asked, "When scientists determine the age of any given rock,
what do they measure?"

"Time," I replied.

"No," he answered. "They measure the ratio of parent isotopes to daughter isotopes. Here's how it works. Unstable parent isotopes deteriorate into steadier daughter isotopes during the radioactive decay process. The ratio of parent to daughter isotopes present in a crystal is governed by elapsed time since radioactive elements and their decay products are locked within a crystal. At each equal increment of time, or half-life, half the parent isotopes decay to daughter isotopes. Ages are calculated by completing a series of mathematical equations I won't bore you with, and by building decay curves.

"Seems technically sound, doesn't it? But hold on. Scientists assume three things when they date rocks. One: no contamination occurs along the way. Two: the initial conditions of the sample. Three: radioactive decay rates remain constant for billions of years. These assumptions stem from what's called uniformitarianism. Do you know what that is, Tim?"

I answered, "No."

"Uniformitarianism is 'a doctrine that assumes processes of the past are essentially the same as those of the present day,'" he explained. "Uniformitarianism is uniformly questionable.[50] Assumptions generate assumed answers.[51] Variables vary things, and rate of change changes everything.[52] Back in 1996, a sample of the lava from the Mt. St. Helens crater was analyzed by scientists using radiometric dating. The results yielded an age of 350,000 years.[53] Problem is, the eruption occurred ten years earlier in 1986. Here's a case where we know when the rock formed, and how old it is, the age was only off 35,000 percent. Doesn't sound like good science to me."

Paul quickly discredited my school's version of natural history, from fossils to the geologic record. However, I still held firm to my beliefs. That was until he put the final nail in the coffin. He contended the greatest argument against Darwinism is the evolutionary tree.

"According to Darwin," he said, "the evolutionary processes produced all bio-diversity on planet earth gradually through a process called natural selection, and that random mutations provide much of the variability needed for natural selection to operate. As time progresses more genetic information gets added and more species develop. In reality, over time, genetic information gets corrupted, or even lost. There are fewer species now than in the past. The evolutionary tree is upside down. If Darwin had come up with the theory of devolution instead of the *Theory of Evolution*, he would've been right."

"All right!" I hollered. "Maybe I don't know as much about evolution as I thought. Maybe it does take faith to believe in it!"

"Certainly," Paul concurred. "I tell you, Tim, it takes a lot less faith to believe *The Rock* created life, than life evolved from a rock, and after a flood creatures repopulated the earth deliberately, than creatures flooded the earth accidentally. Evolution is just a religion, and a ridiculous one at that. The only reason the scientific community doesn't discount it is because of its alternative, special creation. They stay willfully ignorant because they 'cannot allow a divine foot in the door.'"[54]

• • •

Paul's case left little doubt. Evolution was boloney. But I didn't see any connection between evolution and slavery. I asked, "What does evolution have to do with slavery?"

He answered, "Not only was Charles Darwin wrong about geology and biology, he was wrong about humanity. Darwin in *The Descent of Man* wrote this:"

> Man is liable to numerous, slight, and diversified variations, which are induced by the same general causes, are governed and transmitted in accordance with the same general laws, as in the lower animals. Man tends to multiply at so rapid a rate that his offspring are necessarily exposed to a struggle for existence, and consequently to natural selection. He has given rise to many races, some of which are so different that they have often been ranked by naturalists as distinct species.[55]

> Through the means just specified, aided perhaps by others as yet undiscovered, man has been raised to his present state. But since he attained to the rank of manhood, he has diverged into distinct, or as they may be more appropriately called sub-species. Some of these, for instance the Negro and European, are so distinct that, if specimens had been brought to a naturalist without any further information, they would undoubtedly have been considered by him as good and true species.[56]

"Truth is, there's only one specie of man," Paul explained. "Modern scientists, including geneticists, contradict Darwin. Look."

> The Book of Genesis puts Adam and Eve together in the Garden of Eden, but geneticists' version of the duo—the ancestors to whom the Y chromosomes and mitochondrial DNA of today's humans

can be traced—were thought to have lived tens of thousands of years apart. Now, two major studies of modern humans' Y chromosomes suggest that 'Y-chromosome Adam' and 'mitochondrial Eve' may have lived around the same time after all.[57]

The SNPs are believed to be representative of the genome (total human DNA) such that what is true for them would be true for the whole genome. These studies and others have shown that the difference in DNA between any two humans is amazingly low . . . only 0.1 percent.[58]

"Tim, it's as the *Bible* says:"

> God that made the world and all things therein, seeing that he is Lord of heaven and earth, dwelleth not in temples made with hands; Neither is worshipped with men's hands, as though he needed any thing, seeing he giveth to all life, and breath, and all things; And hath made of one blood all nations of men for to dwell on all the face of the earth, and hath determined the times before appointed, and the bounds of their habitation; (Acts 17:24–26 *KJV*)

"Darwin derived his well-known theory from others who didn't know very well. It's pure malarkey. Differences between humans are cosmetic and primarily cultural. Darwin's claim that the races are distinct species is wholly antiquated, as are so many other claims he made."

I was taken aback. I commented, "Charles Darwin is an icon. Nobody told me he was a racist."

"Indeed, he was," Paul replied. "Bet they didn't teach you that in school."

"No," I told him.

He said, "If Darwin is correct, and humans are, indeed, animals, if evolution is in fact true, if there's such a thing as genetic supremacy, and if ethics don't exist, then survival of the fittest applies. It's the law of the jungle, Tim. If Darwinism is real, slavery is as natural as life and death."

I started thinking. *Can there be moral condemnation, if there're no morals? Can somebody really say something is wrong, if nothing is right?* According to Darwin, we're highly evolved animals. Stronger lions kill weaker ones to survive, so why can't we do the same to frailer human beings? Animals aren't jailed for homicide, why are we incarcerated and not them? The thought was troubling. Darwinism's potential, if it was ever unleashed, could be truly horrific.

I said, "It's a good thing Darwin never inspired anyone to commit genocide."

"He did," Paul answered. "Darwin also wrote this in *The Descent of Man*:"

> At some future period, not very distant as measured by centuries, the civilized races of man will almost certainly exterminate and replace throughout the world the savage races. At the same time the anthropomorphous apes, as Professor Schaaffhausen has remarked, will no doubt be exterminated. The break will then be rendered wider, for it will intervene between man in a more civilized state, as we may hope, than the Caucasian, and some ape as low as a baboon, instead of as at present between the negro or Australian and the gorilla.[59]

"Statements like this," he said, "inspired Adolf Hitler. He was one of the world's most notorious dictators. In 1925 he wrote:"

> The stronger must dominate and not mate with the weaker, which would signify the sacrifice of its own higher nature. Only the born weakling can look upon this principle as cruel, and if he does so it is merely because he is of a feebler nature and narrower mind; for if such a law did not direct the process of evolution then the higher development of organic life would not be conceivable at all.[60]

> If Nature does not wish that weaker individuals should mate with the stronger, she wishes even less that a superior race should intermingle with an inferior one; because in such a case all her efforts, throughout hundreds of thousands of years, to establish an evolutionary higher stage of being, may thus be rendered futile.[61]

"You probably know the rest. Adolf Hitler and the Nazis, in an effort to rid Germany of undesirables, killed millions, mostly Jews, during World War II."

I said, "I know about the Holocaust. I had no idea Darwin had anything to do with it."

"He didn't, at least not directly," Paul replied. "What Darwin did is provide justification. Darwin didn't kill anybody during World War II. He wasn't even alive then. The Third Reich initiated the slaughter. Darwin didn't take Europe hostage in 1939 either. He took science hostage decades earlier in 1859. He didn't enslave men in concentration camps. No. He enslaved them to materialism and naturalism. Darwin instituted the idea of natural selection. He didn't select who would take the idea to its natural end."

• • •

Again we turned our attention to the subject of slavery in the United States. Paul said, "Remember when I told you about the amendment process. The institution of slavery officially ended in America in 1865 when the 13th Amendment to the *United States Constitution* was ratified. Read."

> Neither slavery nor involuntary servitude, except as a punishment for crime whereof the party shall have been duly convicted, shall exist within the United States, or any place subject to their jurisdiction.[62]

"Slavery became illegal toward the end of the 19th century, but it took a nasty civil war and unprecedented bloodshed for it to happen. Abolishing the institution wasn't easy. Slavery pitted the Republican North against the Democrat South before the matter was finally resolved."

CHAPTER 3

The First Civil War

Different genes, different nationalities,
different cultures, different nations

OUR CONVERSATION CONTINUED INTO the night passed sundown. Paul told me, "Tensions regarding slavery increased all the more in 1854 after Congress passed *The Kansas–Nebraska Act* and President Pierce signed it into law. The act was so divisive," he said, "a whole new political party formed because of it." He pulled out *Chronicle of America* once again and put it in my hands.

> United in their opposition to slavery, a group of Whigs, Free Soil Democrats and Liberty Party men gathered at a schoolhouse here on February 28 to discuss what actions they would take if the Kansas-Nebraska Act should pass. The group, which had been called together by a local lawyer, Alvan E. Bovay, resolved that if it should pass, they would form a new party. Bovay suggested they call it "Republican," after the party of Thomas Jefferson, who was seen as an opponent of slavery, a champion of the concept of a nation of small landowners and a radical opponent of the established aristocracy.[63]

"Republicans, are you kidding me?" I sneered. "They were a bunch of racists. Everybody knows the Republican Party was the party of rich white people. Democrats cared more about blacks, not to mention women, the poor, and the working class than did Republicans."

"Fair enough," Paul responded. "Republicans deserve criticism, but do you know how they got their reputation?"

"No," I answered.

He said, "Racist Democrats from the South, or Dixiecrats as they were known, became Republicans after civil rights laws were passed in the 1950s and '60s. Many in the South switched their allegiance to the Republican Party, which was seen as more conservative. Republicans became known as racists because of Democrats. It's ironic, if you think about it."

"So you're saying Republicans didn't support slavery?" I commented.

"No, Democrats did," Paul replied. "Northern Protestants, businessmen, professionals, factory workers, and, yes, blacks, made up the Republican Party's base prior to the American Civil War. On the other hand, Democrats had Southern farmers and economic populists as their supporters.

"The two parties were regional and drastically different. Republicans were located mainly in the industrial North. They wanted to abolish slavery. Democrats were largely situated in the agrarian South. They wanted to maintain it. A rift quickly formed between the two opposing regions. An editorial in *The Examiner* printed in 1856 was the first public statement warning that fundamental social and economic differences between North and South might lead to civil conflict.[64] In 1859 that rift suddenly became a chasm when the Mississippi legislature resolved to secede from the Union immediately if a Republican was elected president.[65]

"On November 6, 1860 Mississippi's fears came true. After losing an Illinois US Senate race to Democrat Stephen Douglas two years earlier in 1858, Kentucky-born lawyer and Republican nominee Abraham Lincoln became America's 16th president after he defeated Douglas and two others candidates.

"Calls for succession quickly rang out in the South shortly thereafter. One month later in Charleston, South Carolina, the call to secede hit a climax. Read what happened next."

> As crowds milled about outside, South Carolina political leaders met in St. Andrew's Hall on Meeting Street today and, in just 22 minutes, voted to secede from the union. 'We, the people of South Carolina, in convention assembled, do declare and ordain . . . that the union now subsisting between South Carolina and other states under the name of the United States of America is hereby dissolved.'[66]

"Other pro-slavery states followed suit. One by one they seceded from the Union for about the next six months. By June 8, 1861, with the acquisition of Tennessee, the eleven-state Confederacy made up of seven Southern and four Border States was complete. Keep reading."

> Voters endorsed Tennessee's secession from the union today, making it the 11th state to join the Confederacy, though the state remains sharply divided. Sentiment in east Tennessee counties is strongly pro-union. Jefferson Davis, the acting president of the Confederacy, now heads a government of four border states and seven Deep South states. Fiery South Carolina led the way last December 20, shortly after Abraham Lincoln was elected President. Mississippi followed this January 9. Twelve days later, Davis resigned from the United States Senate, predicting a war 'the like of which men have not seen.' By early March, five other Deep South states had seceded: Florida on January 10, Alabama on January 11, Georgia on January 19, Louisiana on January 26, and Texas on March 2. There was opposition in every state, but it was silenced by those called 'fire-eaters' who were bent on secession. Virginia, the mother commonwealth, reluctantly seceded on April 17. It was joined by Arkansas on May 6 and North Carolina on May 20. Tennessee made the Confederacy complete with its vote today.[67]

I knew about slavery, how it kindled the Civil War, but the role the presidential election of 1860 played wasn't clear to me. I had no idea it set the conflict ablaze. So I asked Paul why politics played such a crucial role.

He answered, "Politics has always been, and remains to be, a major cause of strife, both locally and nationally. Southern Democrats were afraid because their livelihood was in jeopardy. When Abraham Lincoln was elected president, Southerners felt threatened. You see, Tim, wherever ideologies collide, there is a great divide.[68] Any time fifty percent of the population goes in one direction and fifty percent in the other, one hundred percent of the populace is in serious risk of experiencing a major upheaval.[69] Wherever there is frustration, there is sedition.[70]

"The Southern States considered the federal government a danger to slavery, which was vital to their regional economy. Abraham Lincoln embodied the abolitionist movement. The Confederate States had benefited from slavery throughout the years. It was their chief source of revenue, and they didn't want to see it end. The first Republican presidency in the history of the United States in and of itself didn't ignite the Civil War. It was merely a catalyst. Abraham Lincoln's victory in 1860 sparked the inevitable."

His words were educational. After he finished speaking we both went to bed and fell asleep.

· · ·

The next morning after breakfast we resumed our discussion. I asked Paul, "Who fired the first shot, the North or the South?"

He said, "The first shots were fired in South Carolina at Fort Sumter. On April 12, 1861, Confederate General P.G.T. Beauregard commanded his forces around Charleston Harbor to open fire on the Union garrison holding the fort. Read."

> Following a bombardment lasting more than two days, the 73-man United States garrison, led by Major Robert Anderson, has surrendered to General Pierre Beauregard, commander of the Provisional Forces of the Confederate States of America. For several months in both the North and the South, all eyes have been watching the new island fort in Charleston harbor and its beleaguered commander. President Jefferson Davis, the leader of the new Confederate government, had insisted that the federal fort belonged to the fledgling Confederacy.[71]

"Immediately after Lincoln took office the garrison at Fort Sumter was in trouble. Confederate leaders already demanded that US Army forces abandon all facilities in Southern territories. After President Lincoln learned his garrison in Charleston Harbor was running out of food and supplies he decided to send supply ships to help his besieged troopers. South Carolinians viewed Lincoln's action a violation. When Lincoln didn't relent, Confederate forces led by General Beauregard bombarded Fort Sumter into submission before provisions arrived. On April 14th, US Army Major Robert Anderson surrendered the fort to Beauregard. The next day it was in Confederate hands."

I said, "I bet Union soldiers took it back within a week."

"No they didn't," Paul responded. "The fort remained under Confederate control for another four years. It wasn't until February, 1865, following General William T. Sherman's March that it would be in Union hands again. The South continued dominating the North. Confederates won battle after battle, including the battles of Bull Run, Wilson's Creek, Seven Pines, Chattanooga, Antietam, Fredericksburg, Chancellorsville, and Galveston. Fort Sumter was just their first victory. Early on, it wasn't looking good for

Lincoln and the North. Though, amid Union defeat, slavery was delivered a serious blow. Take a look."

> Fulfilling a pledge made last September, President Abraham Lincoln has signed the Emancipation Proclamation, freeing all slaves in Confederate states and radically altering the nature of the war.[72]

I asked Paul to tell me more about *The Emancipation Proclamation*. "It was a presidential proclamation," he explained, "issued by Abraham Lincoln based on his constitutional authority as Commander in Chief directed at states and districts in rebellion. It wasn't a law passed by Congress like the 13th Amendment. Rather, it was a wartime measure decreeing as of January 1, 1863, all slaves in rebellious states 'shall be then, thenceforward, and forever free.' It enabled freed persons enrollment into the United States' armed forces paid services, and ordered the Union Army to 'recognize and maintain the freedom of' ex-slaves. It also provided legal framework for freeing more than three million slaves kept in Confederate-held lands."

"How did it change the trajectory of the war?" I asked.

"Good question," he replied. "Lincoln's goal at the onset on the Civil War was reuniting the Union. The proclamation added to that goal, making the eradication of slavery an additional goal. It was an integral first step toward outlawing slavery in the United States."

I interjected. "I bet that's what turned the tide for the North. Millions of freed slaves joined the Union Army en masse immediately after *The Emancipation Proclamation* was issued and they defeated the South."

"Not exactly," Paul countered. "The momentum shifted on a battlefield in Gettysburg, Pennsylvania on July 3, 1863. See."

> After three days of the bloodiest fighting of the war, the Army of the Potomac has finally scored a decisive victory against its tormentor, the formidable Robert E. Lee and his Army of Northern Virginia. Today, the third day, saw the worst fighting as General Lee sent 14,000 men, under General George Pickett, against the Federal center, where they were repulsed with terrible carnage. Only half of Pickett's men returned to their lines after the charge.[73]

"Lee's attempt to invade the North failed. After that, the Federals began picking up steam. Shortly thereafter on July 4th, Ulysses S. Grant captured Vicksburg, giving the Union complete control of the Mississippi River. Four months later on November 25th, Union forces broke the Confederate siege on the city of Chattanooga forcing General Bragg's army south into Georgia."

"Was that the end of the war?" I asked.

"No, the war went on for another couple of years," Paul reacted. "Within that time period," he said, "the North made further gains against the South. Union forces captured and occupied Meridian Mississippi a city known for industry and storage capability and defeated Nathan Bedford Forrest securing supply lines to Sherman's armies who were marching against Atlanta. Two months later on September 1, 1864 Atlanta Georgia fell, and Sherman's army occupied the city the next day.

"From there the South fell apart. On the 19th of September, Union General Philip Sheridan attacked the Confederate army under Jubal Early near the city of Winchester and drove it southward up the Shenandoah Valley. For the next two months Sheridan and Early's armies battled one another for control of the Shenandoah Valley. On October 19, 1864 Sheridan's army won out. Around the same time Fort Harrison a Confederate stronghold near Richmond, Virginia fell to the Army of the James.

"But perhaps the beginning of the end for the South was when General Sherman's Army of Georgia began its 'March to the Sea.' Sherman's Army arrived at Savannah, Georgia on December 10, 1864. His troopers took Fort McAllister at Savannah and forced Confederate defenders to evacuate the city."

"What about the slaves?" I queried. "Were they liberated?"

"Not yet," Paul said. "Their freedom arrived one month later on January 31, 1865 following the reelection of President Abraham Lincoln. On that day the House passed the 13th Amendment to the *United States Constitution*. I showed you that amendment earlier. It's the piece of legislation that officially ended slavery in America."

I said, "I remember it."

"Unfortunately, the passage of the amendment didn't deter the South," Paul said. "Southern forces kept fighting and the war raged on. Sherman's Army left Savannah February 1, 1865 then headed toward the Carolinas where the war had begun. On February 17th, his army captured Columbia, South Carolina and Confederate defenders fled Charleston."

I interjected. "Charleston? Isn't that where Fort Sumter was located?"

"Yes, Tim," Paul replied. "Good, you're paying attention. Sherman broke South Carolina's back. Fort Sumter was re-occupied April 14, 1865, the same day President Lincoln was assassinated. Less than a week after

Sherman's Army captured Columbia, Wilmington, NC fell to Union soldiers, closing the last important Southern port on the east coast. Shortly thereafter, on March 11th, Sherman's Army occupied Fayetteville, North Carolina.

"Remember Robert E. Lee?" Paul probed. "A Confederate defeat at Five Forks forced him to abandon the Petersburg-Richmond siege lines. The once unstoppable Confederate general had to abandon Petersburg and Richmond on April 2, 1865. He had to move his army west. Union soldiers occupied the two Virginia cities the next day on April 3rd. Lee's problems didn't end there. On April 6th, at the Battle of Sailor's Creek, one-third of Lee's army was cornered and annihilated. Three days later on April 9th, Lee, wanting to discuss terms of surrender, sought General Grant in Appomattox Courthouse, Virginia. Read, Tim."

> General Robert E. Lee met with General Ulysses S. Grant at Appomattox Courthouse today and surrendered the Army of Northern Virginia, thus effectively ending the American Civil War.[74]

"So, the war finally ended!" I declared.

"Just about," Paul replied. "The final battle of the Civil War took place at Palmito Ranch, Texas on May 12, 1865. The Confederates won, but the war was essentially over. The war officially ended June 2, 1865 after General Simon Bolivar Buckner's terms for surrender of the Army of the Trans-Mississippi were agreed to."

• • •

"Wow!" I cried. "It wasn't a quick decisive victory for the North, after all. It was a long and bloody struggle."

"The Civil War was the bloodiest war in US history," Paul retorted. "And slavery was its cause. More Americans died in the Civil War than in every other war combined. Read."

> After four long years, the Civil War has left American society with deep scars that may perhaps never be healed. The war has 'carried mourning to almost every home,' President Lincoln has said, until 'it can almost be said that the heavens are hung in black.' No indisputable figures exist, but it is believed the fighting claimed 360,000 Union and 258,000 Confederate casualties. Even the heroes were scarred by their accomplishments. By 1864, General Ulysses S. Grant's war of attrition had earned him the name 'butcher.' In the words of a Confederate general who helped inflict 12,000

casualties on Grant's army at Cold Harbor, 'This is not war, this is murder.' The North may have paid dearly in human life, but the South has been ravaged to its core. Huge land areas are laid waste and two-thirds of the livestock have been killed. Capital resources are depleted and railroads destroyed. One-quarter of the white male population is dead or maimed and slaves worth $2 billion have been liberated.[75]

"I bet Lincoln stuck it to the South. I bet he made the rebels pay," I said gleefully.

Paul quickly countered, "That's not the case. President Lincoln sought reconciliation for the nation, not retribution. Lincoln stretched his hand to the South. Long before the war ended he issued his Proclamation of Amnesty and Reconstruction on December 8, 1863, which would've pardoned those who participated in the 'existing rebellion' had they taken an oath to the Union. And on March 4, 1865, while being inaugurated for a second term he addressed the war torn country with these words:"

The Almighty has His own purposes. 'Woe unto the world because of offences! for it must needs be that offences come; but woe to that man by whom the offence cometh!' If we shall suppose that American Slavery is one of those offences which, in the providence of God, must needs come, but which, having continued through His appointed time, He now wills to remove, and that He gives to both North and South, this terrible war, as the woe due to those by whom the offence came, shall we discern therein any departure from those divine attributes which the believers in a Living God always ascribe to Him? Fondly do we hope–fervently do we pray– that this mighty scourge of war may speedily pass away. Yet, if God wills that it continue, until all the wealth piled by the bond-man's two hundred and fifty years of unrequited toil shall be sunk, and until every drop of blood drawn with the lash, shall be paid by another drawn with the sword, as was said three thousand years ago, so still it must be said 'the judgments of the Lord, are true and righteous altogether.'

'With malice toward none; with charity for all; with firmness in the right, as God gives us to see the right, let us strive on to finish the work we are in; to bind up the nation's wounds; to care for him who shall have borne the battle, and for his widow, and his orphan—to do all which may achieve and cherish a just, and a lasting peace, among ourselves, and with all nations.[76]

"Lincoln's vision was short-lived. He was assassinated April 15, 1865, in Washington, D.C. at Ford's Theater by actor and Confederate sympathizer, John Wilkes Booth. Reconciliation died along with Abraham Lincoln."

"What are you saying?" I interrupted.

"Radical Republicans in the Congress didn't share Lincoln's compassion or his idea for reconstruction." Paul said, "They wanted to stick it to the South, as you said. Take a look."

> Congressman Thaddeus Stevens, the outspoken and uncompromising Republican abolitionist from Pennsylvania, was named today to head the Committee on Reconstruction in the House. Many Republicans feel that President Johnson is acting too quickly in allowing Southern states to rejoin the union. They also see their majority in the Congress threatened by Democrats from the South.[77]

"Who's President Johnson?" I asked. "I thought Lincoln was president during the Civil War."

"Andrew Johnson was the 17th president of the United States. He was a Democrat," Paul said. "Lincoln chose him as his running mate in 1864 as part of the National Union ticket. He became vice president after Lincoln was reelected. After Lincoln was slain he took over as president.

"To say that President Johnson and Radical Republicans had contempt for one another would be an understatement. Johnson favored quick reestablishment of the seceded states and opposed federal protections for former slaves. Republicans, on the other hand, demanded rebels be treated harshly, and emphasized civil rights for freedmen. Johnson also had a different reconstruction agenda. For one thing he resisted the Fourteenth Amendment, a key piece of legislation which broadened the definition of citizenship giving former slaves 'equal protection' under the law. He also issued a series of proclamations that angered hard core Republicans. Among them was a proclamation in 1868 granting amnesty to persons who directly or indirectly took part in the rebellion, similar to Lincoln's 1863 proclamation.

"Johnson was eventually impeached by the Republican-dominated Congress over a violation of *The Tenure of Office Act* and was acquitted by the Senate by only one vote."

I commented, "I always knew Democrats and Republicans couldn't get along, I had no idea they hated each other for so long. I thought their rivalry began at the end of the twentieth century."

"Oh no," Paul replied. "Democrats and Republicans have been at each other's throats since the Civil War. After the war was over the conflict continued. The two parties had to decide how to handle reconstruction, and they didn't see eye to eye. Johnson was the first reconstruction president. His struggle with House Republicans was merely the beginning. It was the first major dispute in what would become a string of conflicts. The fight between Democrats and Republicans started with slavery and it continued for nearly two centuries.

"Republicans won the first battle. Their idea of reconstruction was adopted over Johnson's. On March 2, 1867, Congress enacted the first Reconstruction Act. It was supplemented later by three related acts. The act divided the South with the exception of Tennessee, into five military districts in which the authority of the army commander was supreme. It also required ratification of the Fourteenth Amendment for reinstatement into the Union.

"After the Civil War was over Republicans had absolute control over the South for the next twelve years. And for six and a half decades they dominated the presidency and control of Congress. Yet, their dominance ended abruptly, with an awful crash."

CHAPTER 4

The New Deal

Uncontrollability gives government
the ability to control.

CRASH? I HAD NO idea what that meant. I said, "Paul, clearly there was bad blood between Democrats and Republicans after the Civil War. How long did it last?"

To my surprise he said, "Bitterness still remains. North and South don't see eye to eye in many ways, though they aren't at war any longer. Differences still persist, even now."

He was right. The two regions were at odds after the Revolution. Northerners initially supported the post-revolutionary government. Southerners by and large didn't. Now they both hate it. I needed to clarify so I said, "What I meant was, when did the hostilities end?"

He said, "Reconstruction was over in 1878. Is that what you mean?"

I replied, "Yes." Then I asked, "Did anything change after Reconstruction?"

He said, "Definitely. Yet America was still a volatile place." I asked him how.

He told me, "Between 1878 and 1899 diseases like yellow fever killed thousands, labor disputes and strikes were rampant, new immigrants flooded the nation, monopolies and trusts formed, and tycoons arose. The American economy grew by leaps and bounds. It was a unique time of industry and invention, the heart of the Gilded Age.

"The early twentieth century was a time of political instability as well. Socialists made inroads just about everywhere, anarchists were a threat, the *Women's Suffrage Movement* heated up, and the Federal Reserve Bank was formed changing economics in this country forever. Not to mention, World War I broke out in Europe in 1914 killing millions worldwide, including many US soldiers. Yet, it was a time of breakthroughs, particularly in travel. The airplane was invented then and the Model T came off the assembly line, giving Americans access to places they've never been before.

"America was more stable in the 1920s. An entirely different course was charted then. Read."

> Warren Gamaliel Harding celebrated his 55th birthday today by winning the presidency. Republicans Harding and running mate Calvin Coolidge, Governor of Massachusetts, easily defeated Democrats James Cox for President and Franklin Roosevelt for Vice President. The party's majority in Congress also rose as voters opted for conservatism. 'America's present need is not heroics but healing; not nostrums but normalcy,' Harding has said.[78]

"Before 1921, for about twenty years US presidents were by and large progressive. Party affiliation didn't matter. Such candidates included Republican Theodore Roosevelt and Democrat Woodrow Wilson."

"Progressive?" I asked. "I never heard that word before."

"You haven't," he said. "Progressives believe government is the only tool for change, that governmental action alone produces political, economic, and social improvement. They think there's only one way to advance and that's through sequential change initiated by government. Harding wasn't a progressive. His approach was different from his predecessors. After he took office he promised to undo many of President Wilson's policies. His administration was conservative and pro-business. He cut federal spending, reduced taxes, and raised tariff rates. He signed *The Budget and Accounting Act of 1921* establishing the General Accounting Office and streamlining the federal budget system.

"Under Harding's guidance the economic picture in America improved. Harding, with help from Secretary of the Treasury Andrew Mellon, was able to cut the federal budget and reduce the tax burden during his first year. GNP rebounded and the unemployment rate dropped measurably in 1922."

I said, "He sounds like a great president."

"Though Harding was successful in many ways," he said, "his presidency was marred by the notorious *Teapot Dome* scandal."

"What's that?" I asked.

"It was a corruption scandal," he answered. "The Harding administration was accused of misconduct. Congress investigated it for allegedly issuing fraudulent leases without competitive bidding and for receiving bribes in return."

"Did the scandal bring him down?" I asked.

"It didn't," Paul replied. "Harding died in office before the full extent of any wrongdoing was determined."

I said, "I don't understand."

"Harding's tenure as president was short," Paul answered. "He died in California on August 3, 1923 two years after he was elected while traveling on a tiring transcontinental trip."

• • •

That got me thinking. *If he died, I wondered if his reforms died with him.* I asked Paul, "Did the nation return to progressive politics?"

He said, "No. Calvin Coolidge, Harding's vice president was sworn in while he was on vacation in Vermont on his family's farmhouse the night Harding died. He took over as president. Coolidge, or 'Silent Cal' as he was known, because he was a man of few words maintained Harding's laissez-faire policies. America spurred on. Read."

> . . . Epitomizing his free enterprise philosophy, 'Silent Cal' called for tax reductions in today's speech. He also reiterated his support for the World Court and repayment of war debts by the Allies, and declared his belief that America should distance itself from the League of Nations.[79]

"Coolidge restored the public's confidence in government. He changed the atmosphere in Washington, D.C. He was seen as someone who 'embodied the spirit and hopes of the middle class.'"[80]

"A man of the people," I commented.

"I guess you could say that," Paul replied. "He stayed out of the way. That's why he was so popular. He was actively inactive."

I asked, "What do you mean by that?"

He said, "He was on top, but he didn't topple the economy. He was determinately against fatalism, allowing people to determine their own fate.

He was accessible to everyone, yet he didn't give top-heavy government access to everything. He only did what was necessary, which is necessary for growth.

"While he was president America took off. The country experienced sustained economic growth and prosperity during his tenure. Some called it the 'Coolidge Prosperity.' The roaring '20s as it became known was a time of unprecedented industrial growth and expansion, and a period in which America underwent unparalleled shifts in culture. From 1923 to 1929 the US experienced a renaissance. Automobiles and telephones gained wide usage. Electricity came to many communities. Women acquired the right to vote, and motion pictures entertained the masses.

"Not only that," he said, "it was during this era that the United States emerged as an economic powerhouse. From August 2, 1923 to March 4, 1929 the stock market climbed 225 points, or an astonishing 255 percent. America was awash with money. She lent it out and gained clout worldwide."

I told him, "You mentioned 'an awful crash.' None of this sounds awful to me."

He said, "Please, let me finish. Coolidge was successful by any standard. America grew substantially while he was president. Coolidge was well-liked. On November 4, 1924 he was handily reelected. Look."

> Since assuming the presidency when Harding died, Calvin Coolidge has won the hearts of many Americans with his wry wit and calm manner. Today, he won their votes for President with his laissez-faire policies and catchy campaign slogan, 'Keep Cool With Coolidge.' . . . Coolidge's radio address yesterday helped seal the triumph, as 30 million Americans listened. The election demonstrated the public's desire to let American business run its course with little government regulation. As Coolidge said when nominated, 'America wouldn't be America if the people were shackled with government monopolies.'[81]

"On the surface all seemed well," he said, "but there's more."

• • •

"By 1928 the market began to overheat," Paul explained. "People took advantage of pro-growth policies enacted during the Harding-Coolidge era. Quick money flooded banks and investment firms, and loans for buying stocks with less cash were simple to acquire. Wall Street was awash with inexperienced investors. Big easy profits attracted unseasoned stakeholders. On September 3, 1929, the market reached its peak of 381.17 points.

"Signs began to emerge on Black Thursday. On October 24, 1929, the market was a bubble. Five days later on October 29th, that bubble burst. See for yourself, Tim."

> The stock market has collapsed in a 'Black Tuesday' of violent trading that was the most disastrous in Wall Street history. It was the worst by three key measurements, total losses, total turnover and the number of speculators ruined. Frantic efforts to stabilize the market were met by 'must sell' orders to liquidate at any price, accelerated by insistent brokers' calls for more cash to back the record loans behind the falling stocks.[82]

"Herbert Hoover the Republican president at the time took much of the blame."

I said, "Herbert Hoover? You said Calvin Coolidge was president!"

Paul said, "Sorry, Tim, apparently I left him out. Coolidge chose not to run for a second term in 1928. Hoover was Secretary of Commerce under presidents Harding and Coolidge. He was elected over Democrat Al Smith November 6, 1928 in a landslide victory. Sadly for him, the crash came seven months after he took office."

"Was it his fault?" I asked.

"No, not really," Paul said. "He wasn't responsible for the meltdown, but his erratic policies didn't help. They actually made things worse. Shortly after the market crash Hoover signed a 160 million dollar tax cut hoping the money would be pumped back into the economy. And in 1930 in a complete reversal, he sought approval from Congress for an emergency jobs program that appropriated 116 million dollars to put unemployed people back to work on emergency construction projects. In 1931, in his State of the Union message, he called for a 500 million dollar emergency reconstruction program to aid businesses. Finally, in 1932, he signed a bill creating *The Reconstruction Finance Corporation*, which dispensed 500 million dollars in loans to failing firms.

"Nothing he did worked. His policies were inconsistent and ineffective. In the end the federal government was unable to help. On its own, it couldn't get the struggling US economy back on its feet.

"The *Great Depression* ensued. Consumer spending and industrial output plummeted. Millions lost work and, in many cases, entire economic sectors were devastated. Needless to say, investments dried up, banks failed, and foreclosures became an epidemic. Confidence evaporated along with the nation's spirit."

. . .

My teachers hated capitalism. They argued capitalism only benefitted the rich. I told him, "See all this goes to show my teachers were right. Capitalists are no good."

With a concerned look Paul said, "Capitalism is as good or as bad as those who utilize it,[83] Remember when I told you about the human heart?"

"Yeah," I answered.

"That's the problem," he charged. "Broken people break everything." Paul picked up the *Bible* and read.

> For I know that in me (that is, in my flesh,) dwelleth no good thing: for to will is present with me; but how to perform that which is good I find not. For the good that I would I do not: but the evil which I would not, that I do. Now if I do that I would not, it is no more I that do it, but sin that dwelleth in me. I find then a law, that, when I would do good, evil is present with me. (Romans 7:18–21 *KJV*)

"Capitalism didn't cause the crash," he claimed. "It was man's sinful nature, his greediness, in particular. Capitalism is an economic system. It's a means."

"A means to what?" I asked.

"A means for producing and distributing commodities and other stuffs based on private ownership and competition," he replied.

Without even thinking I said, "Well, it causes havoc. All the inequity in the world is a result of capitalism."

I immediately realized something. For some reason I reacted viscerally every time Paul contradicted the public school system. As soon as he mentioned capitalism, I responded with scorn because my teachers scorned it. When we discussed evolution, it was the same thing. A light came on. I thought *Maybe I should listen*. Perhaps he had information the school system doesn't, or facts it didn't want me to hear. I stopped rebuking him whenever he opposed my formal education, and I just let him talk. After a brief pause I said, "Sorry, Paul, please resume. Tell me why capitalism had nothing to do with the crash."

He said, "Okay. 'The love of money is evil, not money itself.' Remember? Making money isn't evil, making it your god is.[84] Stock traders and slave traders made the same mistake."

"And what's that?" I asked.

"They were guided by avarice instead of rectitude," he answered.

• • •

Moments ago he said capitalism didn't cause the crash. Now he was saying capitalists made a mistake. I was a confused. That sounded contradictory. I asked, "If capitalists caused the crash, how is capitalism blameless?"

"You're equating capitalists with capitalism," he said. "Capitalists are people, and capitalism is 'an economic system.' People were to blame. They took advantage of the system. Capitalism is based upon freedom, as opposed to socialism, which centers on a collective. In a capitalist system individuals are free to buy and sell as they please with limited government oversight. It's a system guided by supply and demand."

I asked him to explain. "Supply and demand," he said, "is a free market economic model. It was in use here in America before the Revolution."

"How did it work?" I probed.

"Simple," he said. "The interaction between supply of a resource and the demand for that resource determined price. The lower the supply and the higher the demand, the higher the price. Contrarily, the greater the supply and the lower the demand, the lower the price."

I said, "Please expound? The whole supply and demand concept baffles me. It isn't clear. How did it affect price?"

"Price was determined by availability and affordability by price," he explained. "Anything with value has a price, Tim. Something no one will pay for has no value, and something no one can pay for has no price. Free market economies were directed by something called the *Invisible Hand*."

I asked, "What's that?"

He said, "The *Invisible Hand* is a term Adam Smith, the eighteenth century Scottish philosopher and political economist, used to describe the self-regulating behavior of the marketplace. It just so happens I have a copy of *The Wealth of Nations* written by Smith right here. See for yourself."

> . . . led by an invisible hand to promote an end which was no part of his intention. Nor is it always the worse for the society that it was no part of it. By pursuing his own interest he frequently

promotes that of the society more effectually than when he really intends to promote it.[85]

"The *Invisible Hand* is essentially an unseen force or mechanism. It guides individuals to unwittingly benefit society through the pursuit of their private interests." He gave me an illustration. "Say, for example, there's a coat maker and he's in need of money. And say there're individuals without coats. That coat maker in a free market capitalist system can produce coats for profit and individuals are free to buy them to stay warm in that same system. The coat maker is driven by gain and the individuals by necessity. Each is aided by the other's own self-interest.

"Say another coat maker comes along. He manufactures coats cheaper. Additional coats are accessible now, and more individuals can buy them because they cost less. Demand drives innovation and competition keeps prices down."

Everything he said made perfect sense. What he said next made even more. "With freedom comes responsibility. Freedom without temperance is anarchy, and anarchy is the first step toward tyranny.[86] In the 1920s, Americans were freer. Government stayed out of the way. Entrepreneurs and investors weren't kept on such a tight leash. Paradoxically, the freedoms that existed back then contributed to the imprisonment we're experiencing now."

I said, "How so?"

"Economies are fueled by need, not by greed,"[87] Paul answered. "The roaring twenties was a time of freedom; it was also a period of excess. The *Invisible Hand* really wasn't at work before the crash. Gluttony for the most part fueled the market's growth, not demand. Once dividends started coming in, stockholders couldn't get enough. You see, Tim, insatiability is the road to insufficiency.[88] He who always wants money is always in want of money.[89] Being poor is the ultimate end, if being rich is the ultimate goal.[90] The crash occurred because Wall Street created a bubble. Investors purchased stocks on margin. They borrowed for the purpose of gaining financial leverage, and nobody stopped them. Many Americans assumed the market would always go up, so they mortgaged homes and invested their life savings into stocks not even worth the paper they were written on. Many were defrauded out of their hard earned money because what they were investing in wasn't even in demand. They bought into a dream instead of reality. When the market crashed, unsuspecting shareholders were left holding the bag.

"The situation in America in the 1920s was a lot like a prince waiting to be king." He gave me an analogy.

> A prince was told he would be king. This prince lived excessively until the day his father died because he believed it was his right to become king. He acquired land and other goods and made agreements as if he was already ruler.
>
> The prince didn't know his mother the queen already made arrangements for his brother to become king. When the time had come for the new king to take his seat, the prince saw someone else sitting on the throne. To say the least, the prince was distraught; he was left holding debt without any means of paying it off.[91]

"Quick bucks go out just as quickly as they come in," he said.[92] "What is built quickly falls quickly, and what takes no time to build tumbles in no time.[93] The fat man becomes a lean man when the fat man is not a keen man.[94] Wantonness leaves men in want.[95]

"Whatever caused the crash, something had to be done about it, and something was. On November 8, 1932 the first nail in liberty's coffin was driven. Independence for many years brought dependence for many more, after a 'new' president was elected."

· · ·

We both heard guards approaching. Paul immediately put away his books and sat. He said, "They're doing their rounds. Sit tight. Most of the time they just walk up and down the hallway. Sometimes they enter the cell, but that's pretty rare. They'll be gone before you know it." It was about noon and it was my first full day in the HSW. Paul took the intrusion in stride, but I was scared. He could tell I was nervous.

"This happens every day about the same time," he said. "Relax." The guards cruised the corridor for a half hour or so. Finally, as they approached the exit I heard their footsteps get fainter. "See I told you. Nothing to worry about," Paul announced. I asked him if it was safe to talk. "Sure," he answered.

Then I said, oh, so quietly, "We left off at 'the first nail in liberty's coffin,' and 'a new president.' Tell me more."

"That's right!" he reacted. "I don't want to leave you hanging. Let's continue. The first step out of the *Great Depression* toward America's complete and total subjugation happened three years after the market crashed. The number of Americans out of work stood in the millions. According to the chairman of President Hoover's Emergency Committee for Employment, rampant unemployment represented a 'social danger.' In response to the crisis, Democrats fielded a progressive candidate named Franklin Delano Roosevelt to run against Hoover. On November 8, 1932, he was elected the 32nd president of the United States in an enormous victory. Look for yourself."

> When Franklin D. Roosevelt exclaimed at the Democratic conven-
> tion that he 'pledged a new deal for the American people,' they
> believed him—and took their beliefs to the polls. In an election
> that many experts consider the most crucial since Lincoln's victory
> more than 70 years ago, Roosevelt has been swept into the White
> House with an overwhelming plurality.[96]

"Roosevelt trounced Hoover. He garnered 57 percent of the popular vote to Hoover's 39 percent. He won 42 out of 48 states, including the
former Confederate States, and acquired 472 electoral votes. Hoover only
gained 59. It was a blowout."

"Roosevelt must've been a great candidate," I commented.

"He was the perfect candidate for the time," Paul replied. "Three things
helped him breeze into office. One: anxiety over the economy; two: linger-
ing animosity for Republicans in the South; three: populism."

I said, "His message had to be big for him to win so big."

"Roosevelt didn't promise much on the campaign trail," Paul said,
"other than the 'new deal to the American people' he swore in his Chicago
acceptance speech. He never specified what that meant, and for the most
part Americans didn't ask. They just went to the polls out of frustration.
They trusted a man with a slogan to get the nation out of its malaise."

I told him, "You, yourself, said, something needed to be done, and
that Hoover's policies 'made things worse.' Why wouldn't they elect a new
leader?" At first it sounded like he agreed, but once again, his words were
unexpected.

"Hoover was an awful president. That's true. His administration
didn't deserve a second term. The question wasn't whether Hoover was
good or bad, but if Roosevelt was better or worse. Voters didn't vet 'the
New Deal.' They had no idea what it meant, or if it was even good for the
country. See, Tim, you can't replace bad incumbents with good mantras.
The American people had no idea what they were getting themselves into.
It wasn't until Roosevelt was sworn in as president that 'the New Deal' was
brought to light."

I joked, "Please illuminate, no pun intended."

"Okay," he said. "On March 4, 1933 Roosevelt's plan was finally exposed. While taking the oath of office he said this:"

> It is to be hoped that the normal balance of Executive and legislative authority may be wholly adequate to meet the unprecedented task before us. But it may be that an unprecedented demand and need for undelayed action may call for temporary departure from that normal balance of public procedure.
>
> I am prepared under my constitutional duty to recommend the measures that a stricken Nation in the midst of a stricken world may require. These measures, or such other measures as the Congress may build out of its experience and wisdom, I shall seek, within my constitutional authority, to bring to speedy adoption.
>
> But in the event that the Congress shall fail to take one of these two courses, and in the event that the national emergency is still critical, I shall not evade the clear course of duty that will then confront me.[97]

"He then asked Congress, 'For the one remaining instrument to meet the crisis—broad executive power to wage a war against the emergency, as great as the power that would be given to me if we were in fact invaded by a foreign foe.'[98] 'The New Deal' finally had significance after Roosevelt's first inaugural speech. It was statism."

I asked, "What's statism?"

"It's concentration of economic controls and planning in the hands of a highly centralized government," Paul answered. "Roosevelt wanted to sow the seeds of big government, and did. After Roosevelt's victory in 1932 America had a new god different from the One mentioned in the *Declaration of Independence*. In a time of unrest, when America needed God most, she turned to a new god: government. The ancient Israelites did the same thing in their time of need. Once their judges 'turned aside after lucre, and took bribes, and perverted judgment' they sought a king. Read."

> And his sons walked not in his ways, but turned aside after lucre, and took bribes, and perverted judgment. Then all the elders of Israel gathered themselves together, and came to Samuel unto Ramah, And said unto him, Behold, thou art old, and thy sons walk not in thy ways: now make us a king to judge us like all the nations. But the thing displeased Samuel, when they said, Give us a king

to judge us. And Samuel prayed unto the LORD. And the LORD said unto Samuel, Hearken unto the voice of the people in all that they say unto thee: for they have not rejected thee, but they have rejected me, that I should not reign over them. According to all the works which they have done since the day that I brought them up out of Egypt even unto this day, wherewith they have forsaken me, and served other gods, so do they also unto thee. (1 Samuel 8:3–8 *KJV*)

"God warned the Israelites through the prophet Samuel, explaining to them the nature of the king that would bear rule. Samuel issued an admonition from the Lord:"

And he said, This will be the manner of the king that shall reign over you: He will take your sons, and appoint them for himself, for his chariots, and to be his horsemen; and some shall run before his chariots. And he will appoint him captains over thousands, and captains over fifties; and will set them to ear his ground, and to reap his harvest, and to make his instruments of war, and instruments of his chariots. And he will take your daughters to be confectionaries, and to be cooks, and to be bakers. And he will take your fields, and your vineyards, and your oliveyards, even the best of them, and give them to his servants. And he will take the tenth of your seed, and of your vineyards, and give to his officers, and to his servants. And he will take your menservants, and your maidservants, and your goodliest young men, and your asses, and put them to his work. He will take the tenth of your sheep: and ye shall be his servants. And ye shall cry out in that day because of your king which ye shall have chosen you; and the LORD will not hear you in that day. (1 Samuel 8:11–18 *KJV*)

"Were they oppressed?" I asked.

"Indeed," Paul replied. "The Israelites didn't heed God's warning. Consequently, they lost freedom soon after they lost God. For four and a half centuries they were under a monarch's thumb, just as God had foretold, and for twenty-five centuries, they were governed by unsympathetic foreigners. It wasn't until 1948 after God restored Israel that the nation was free once again. It took about three thousand years to break the yoke. Eventually, the tyrants disappeared."

• • •

"America didn't learn from ancient Israel," Paul remarked. "Roosevelt, much like a king, came out swinging. It didn't take long for him to flex his muscles. Days into his first term he circumvented Congress. He bypassed the legislative process, and acted unilaterally. Take a look."

> Roosevelt's first official act two days after taking office on March 4 was to issue an emergency executive order that temporarily closed all the nation's banks to stop the massive 'runs' that threatened to destroy the entire banking system, and to buy time for their reorganization.[99]

"Shortly thereafter Roosevelt and the Congress enacted first-of-its-kind legislation. Look again."

> Calling Congress into special session, he then pushed through numerous and significant—some would say revolutionary pieces of legislation. On March 31, Congress established the Civilian Conservation Corps. FDR had the legislators abandon the gold standard on April 19. On May 12, he pressed Congress to enact the Federal Emergency Relief Act, which set up a national relief system; the Agricultural Adjustment Act, which set a national farm policy, and the Emergency Farm Mortgage Act, which enabled farmers to refinance their farms. In another whirlwind of legislative actions, Roosevelt and Congress enacted the Truth-in-Securities Act, which called for full disclosure in the issuance of new securities, the National Industrial Recovery Act, which provided for industry codes guaranteeing fair labor practices, and the Glass-Steagall Act, which among its other provisions, guaranteed bank deposits.[100]

"Of all this legislation Harold Ickes Roosevelt's Secretary of the Interior said, 'It's more than a New Deal. It's a new world.'[101] Roosevelt didn't stop there. On August 14, 1935 in Washington, D.C., his most notable legislative accomplishment became law. Read."

> President Roosevelt signed into law today one of the most important pieces of legislation in American history, the Social Security Act. It provides a pension to Americans over the age of 65 (beginning in 1942), paid for by contributions from employee wages and matched by employers. It also gives assistance to the blind and disabled and to dependent children. At the same time, it establishes a system of unemployment compensation. Glowing with pride because the act fulfills a campaign promise, the President called the legislation the 'cornerstone' of the New Deal . . .[102]

"Within two short years America was a welfare state. It wasn't intended to be pseudo socialist, but with his new unprecedented powers Roosevelt made it happen quite precipitously."

"Are you saying Roosevelt was a king," I responded, "that he had no opposition at all?"

"No, that's not what I'm saying," he replied. "Roosevelt had opponents. Several key pieces of his 'New Deal' legislation were struck down as unconstitutional by the United States Supreme Court during his first administration. But a frustrated Roosevelt in kinglike manner proposed expanding the number of justices on the Court. Many Americans saw that as court packing and rejected the endeavor outright. The plan was rebuffed by Congress immediately after it was proposed, and Roosevelt was handily defeated."

"So, why then are you lambasting him?" I cried out. "If all he wanted to do was help, why are you attacking him? I don't understand. Is helping others a bad thing?"

"You're right, Tim," Paul replied. "Helping others isn't a bad thing at all. It just depends on how you go about doing it?"

I said with aggravation, "Sounds like the nation needed help, I understand why Roosevelt did what he did. I don't understand why you're so critical of him."

"Methodology matters," he countered. He gave me a comparison.

> A rancher with a rodent problem thought to himself, vipers eat rats, they might help. One day the rancher gathered some vipers together, and he let them go in his field. The next morning he learned his plan failed; he still had a rodent problem, but now things were worse—the vipers had poisoned his livestock.[103]

"Yeah, yeah," I said, nodding. "Rats and vipers, for once could you, please, just spit it out?"

"Okay," he said. "The rancher represents Roosevelt, the rats represent greedy bankers, and the vipers, they represent statism. Statism is worse than any banker we could face. It has unintended consequences. More often than not, it doesn't even alleviate the trouble we're in. It just adds more trouble to a preexisting list of troubles. Roosevelt didn't end the *Great Depression*. World War II did that. The only thing Roosevelt did was increase the scope and size of government. Look around you! Tell me, do you love big out of control government?"

The answer to that, an emphatic no! It finally sunk in. Paul wasn't as-sailing the *New Deal* because of its ends, but because of its means.

He said, "The *New Deal* was, indeed, the start of something new, dependency."

"Dependency on what?" I asked.

"Dependency on government," he replied. "The *New Deal* gave government 'new' power—power to take from one, and power to give to another. Before the *New Deal* the United States government couldn't do that. What happened in America in 1932 was a lot like what happened in Egypt almost four thousand years ago." Paul handed me the *Bible* and told me to read.

> And when money failed in the land of Egypt, and in the land of Canaan, all the Egyptians came unto Joseph, and said, Give us bread: for why should we die in thy presence? for the money faileth. And Joseph said, Give your cattle; and I will give you for your cattle, if money fail. And they brought their cattle unto Joseph: and Joseph gave them bread in exchange for horses, and for the flocks, and for the cattle of the herds, and for the asses: and he fed them with bread for all their cattle for that year. When that year was ended, they came unto him the second year, and said unto him, We will not hide it from my lord, how that our money is spent; my lord also hath our herds of cattle; there is not ought left in the sight of my lord, but our bodies, and our lands: Wherefore shall we die before thine eyes, both we and our land? buy us and our land for bread, and we and our land will be servants unto Pharaoh: and give us seed, that we may live, and not die, that the land be not desolate. And Joseph bought all the land of Egypt for Pharaoh; for the Egyptians sold every man his field, because the famine prevailed over them: so the land became Pharaoh's. And as for the people, he removed them to cities from one end of the borders of Egypt even to the other end thereof. Only the land of the priests bought he not; for the priests had a portion assigned them of Pharaoh, and did eat their portion which Pharaoh gave them: wherefore they sold not their lands. Then Joseph said unto the people, Behold, I have bought you this day and your land for Pharaoh: lo, here is seed for you, and ye shall sow the land. And it shall come to pass in the increase, that ye shall give the fifth part unto Pharaoh, and four parts shall be your own, for seed of the field, and for your food, and for them of your households, and for

food for your little ones. And they said, Thou hast saved our lives: let us find grace in the sight of my lord, and we will be Pharaoh's servants. (Genesis 47:15–25 *KJV*)

"Permanent constituencies are created by permanent dependencies.[104] Entitlements enlist enslavements, and handouts hand out subjugation.[105] Reliant men are compliant men."[106] Paul asked, "Is it really humane to yoke someone to the federal government?"

I said, "No."

"That's exactly what Roosevelt did!" he shouted.

• • •

Maybe government isn't the answer. All too often we believe it is our salvation, when in fact it is our oppressor. Why do we believe our jailors are our liberators? All I had to do was look around to see Paul was right. I'm in a federal prison, and America is imprisoned by feds. If he was wrong, it wouldn't be that way. If I was free, I wouldn't be in this awful place, and if America was free, the feds wouldn't place awful restrictions on everyone. Roosevelt is lauded as a hero. Maybe we ought to rethink everything. There's nothing heroic about the situation we're in.

• • •

I asked, "What became of Roosevelt? What happened after the *New Deal*?"

Paul said, "The Depression eased in 1939 and by 1941 it was over. Roosevelt, like the Pharaoh in Egypt, was popular. He was re-elected three times. On April 12, 1945, he died in office, but his legacy lived on.

CHAPTER 5

Happy Days

People at ease are easily herded.

I SAID, "OBVIOUSLY, AMERICA had a change of fortune. Was the *New Deal* responsible?"

Paul said, "Absolutely. For better or worse, America was different after the *New Deal*. See for yourself."

> When the late President Roosevelt initiated the G.I. Bill in November 1942, he asked for quick congressional action. He got it and signed the bill into law a year and a half later. Now, more than four million veterans of the war are taking advantage of the housing, business and educational opportunities it has afforded.[107]

"The *New Deal* moved America in an entirely 'new' direction," he explained.

I asked, "How?"

"There was a mass exodus away from farms into cities to corporations because of it," he alluded. "Once World War II was over, people returned to work, including many veterans. They married, formed new families, and ultimately they headed for the suburbs. Like the Egyptians who four thousand years earlier left property and sovereignty in exchange for guaranteed security, they left hard independent lives for easier ones."

I began to think. *Modern America and ancient Egypt? I never thought the two were similar.* Paul had revealed something I hadn't known. The ancient world and the modern world really aren't that different. *There's nothing new under the sun*, I realized.

He said, "The *New Deal* changed many things. It changed the American dream itself."

I told him, "I don't understand."

He said, "Before the Depression the American dream meant freedom from tyranny. After it was over, it quickly became freedom from hardship. People had significantly more free time and a lot less to worry about after the *New Deal*, mainly because Roosevelt's programs had backstopped them. With all his new safety nets in place, fewer Americans had to struggle to survive."

"That doesn't sound like a bad thing to me," I alleged.

"In and of itself, it isn't," Paul responded. "The problem was with more time on their hands, and less stress, the American people grew comfortable and secure. Ultimately they 'waxed fat' like ancient Israel. From there trouble brewed."

• • •

I thought *This I have to hear.* Paul pulled out the *Bible* and began to explain. "About seventy years after God brought the children of Israel out of Egypt they settled into the land of Canaan. They were filled and became fat. Look here," he said.

> So the children went in and possessed the land, and thou subduedst before them the inhabitants of the land, the Canaanites, and gavest them into their hands, with their kings, and the people of the land, that they might do with them as they would. And they took strong cities, and a fat land, and possessed houses full of all goods, wells digged, vineyards, and oliveyards, and fruit trees in abundance: so they did eat, and were filled, and became fat, and delighted themselves in thy great goodness. (Nehemiah 9:24–25 *KJV*)

"God warned the Israelites through His servant Moses, this very thing would happen. Moses wrote:"

> Butter of kine, and milk of sheep, with fat of lambs, and rams of the breed of Bashan, and goats, with the fat of kidneys of wheat; and thou didst drink the pure blood of the grape. But Jeshurun waxed fat, and kicked: thou art waxen fat, thou art grown thick, thou art covered with fatness; then he forsook God which made him, and

lightly esteemed the Rock of his salvation. They provoked him to jealousy with strange gods, with abominations provoked they him to anger. They sacrificed unto devils, not to God; to gods whom they knew not, to new gods that came newly up, whom your fathers feared not. Of the Rock that begat thee thou art unmindful, and hast forgotten God that formed thee. (Deuteronomy 32:14–18 KJV)

The next thing he said was odd: "Blessings can be a curse." I asked him to expound. He told me, "Possessions breed obsessions, and obsessions spawn transgressions.[108] After the Israelites left the desert and came into the Promised Land, their needs were immediately filled. As soon as they were satisfied, their hearts were lifted. Read."

Yet I am the LORD thy God from the land of Egypt, and thou shalt know no god but me: for there is no saviour beside me. I did know thee in the wilderness, in the land of great drought. According to their pasture, so were they filled; they were filled, and their heart was exalted; therefore have they forgotten me. (Hosea 13:4–6 KJV)

"They no longer needed God, or so they thought. The desert was behind them. In front was the land of milk and honey. Once the hardship was over, the same God who blessed them became a distant memory. America was similar after World War II."

I asked, "In what way?"

"The United States was in better shape economically," Paul claimed. "Politically, it had been systematically transformed. Government's role was a lot different after the *New Deal*, and so was God's for that matter. With the Depression in the rear view mirror, and government guaranteed security lying ahead, the American people soon became self-centered instead of God-centered."

I said, "And your point is?"

"Metal is forged in a furnace and storms replenish soil," he said. "It's easy to get distracted when all is well, and there're no trials and tribulations. Hearts harden easily in easy times. Material things distract us from things that are important—things like family, friends, and God. There were copious distractions after World War II. In 1946 the biggest distraction of all came along."

• • •

Before I could utter another sentence Paul said, "I'm sure you want to know what distraction I'm referring to."

"You bet!" I responded.

He announced, "After World War II ended America was introduced to the prophet. This prophet appeared in the late 1800s, was miniaturized in 1927, and made its way into American homes in 1946. Do you have any idea what I'm referring to?"

"No I don't! Out with it!" I told him.

"Okay," he reacted. "It's the television set. People started flocking to motion pictures, or 'flickers' as they were called back then at the end of the nineteenth century. Read."

> 'Movies' or 'flickers' are becoming one of the biggest things in the entertainment industry, largely as a result of inventions by the Lumiere brothers in France and Thomas A. Edison here.[109]

"Television evolved from 'flickers' in 1927. On September 7th that same year a 21-year-old inventor by the name of Philo Taylor Farnsworth successfully demonstrated the first electronic television in San Francisco, California. Years later RCA licensed Farnsworth's idea and started producing the first five by twelve inch television sets. At first television sets were primitive and the buyers few. As time progressed the technology improved, and so did the number of TV stations. By 1949, twenty two years after the first TV was invented, the number of Americans who lived within range of these stations grew, and so did the market. The number of televisions used in American homes rose from 6000 in 1946 when the device first came out, to 12 million in 1951. By 1955 half of all US households had one. The prophet has been on the rise ever since. Needless to say, the number of people under its spell is now astronomical."

"That's for sure," I responded. "This prophet, as you say, is everywhere. You can't get away from it. It's in our homes. It's out on the streets. It's in our pockets. It's even in this lousy prison! Even when I want to get away from it, I can't."

Paul chuckled. "Like I said, 'Distraction.' There were other prophets before the television set—books, newspapers and magazines, and radio, for example, but none of them captivated the public, or galvanized the masses as did TV. Do you know why television was so successful?" he asked. I told him I didn't.

He said, "It was suburban life."

I asked, "How so?"

"Life was easier after the *New Deal*," he said. "There weren't chickens to feed anymore, cows to milk, seeds to plant, or crops to reap come harvest time. 'There was a mass exodus away from farms into cities.' Remember? Nine to five jobs became the norm. At the end of the workday most people retired to tiny apartments or small family homes. There was nothing for them to do between five and ten p.m. For those five hours they were bored. They couldn't live it up. They had to get up for work the next day. They couldn't tackle anything strenuous either. Why? Because they'd already worked an eight-hour shift. Television was the perfect filler. It provided amusement with no effort whatsoever.

"The 1950s was the decade of the TV icon," he said as he shrugged his shoulders. "Super stars such as Marilyn Monroe and Elvis Presley fascinated American audiences as never before. Look for yourself," he insisted.

> She is Fox's biggest box-office draw and Hollywood's newest sex goddess: Marilyn Monroe, 29. She wiggles, she pouts, she speaks in a husky, whispery voice and exudes a both inviting and wholesome sensuality with equal parts of reality and humor.[110]

> Elvis Presley is a phenomenon. Music critics call him 'unspeakably untalented and vulgar,' a clergyman branded him 'a whirling dervish of sex' and business boomed for a Cincinnati car dealer who promised to smash 50 Presley records for each customer. But while adults recoil in horror from the 21-year-olds high energy pelvic gyrations and defiant sneer, delirious teenage fans bought seven million copies of his records this year.[111]

"Have you ever heard the term *cult of personality* before?" he asked. I hadn't, so I said no. He explained the term. "Cult of personality is when individuals or groups use propaganda on mass media to create an idealized and oftentimes worshipful image of themselves. It was used by emperors back in ancient times and communists in more modern times. However, after TV, this practice became easy. Every image, word, or action could be planned out ahead of time and filmed later by cameras. After the TV was invented, sanitizing messages became quite simple. Early on people knew television would play a significant role in American society, including politics. In 1927 as soon as the TV was demonstrated this was said:"

> The first public demonstration in America of the new invention television has shown its potential not only as an entertainment medium, but as a political tool.[112]

"Three decades later in 1960 that prediction became a reality. On September 26th Republican Vice President Richard Nixon squared off against Massachusetts Democratic Senator John F. Kennedy in the first ever televised presidential debate. Going into the debate Nixon, a seasoned politician, led Kennedy, the younger lesser known candidate, in the polls. After the debate, the polls changed. Read."

> The great presidential television debates have ended, and according to the Gallup Poll, Senator John F. Kennedy is the winner. Going into the series of four all-network programs, Gallup had Vice President Richard M. Nixon leading, 47 to 46, with 7 percent undecided. Coming out, it's Kennedy on top, 51 to 45, with 4 percent on the fence. Political pundits and television critics alike believe that most of the shift came as early as the first of the four debates. They say both men handled themselves well, but they think Kennedy just looked better on the tube.[113]

"Most listeners who heard the debate on the radio said it was a draw, or that Nixon was the victor. The 70 million plus television viewers on the other hand overwhelmingly said Kennedy won. The difference was TV. Nixon was recovering from a knee injury, was underweight and sweaty because he had the flu, and he wore no make-up on screen. Kennedy was poised, vibrant, and telegenic, not to mention tan. He wore make-up and didn't blend in with the background the way Nixon did. All this gave Kennedy the edge."

I asked Paul what happened next.

He said, "After the first debate the two candidates had three more debates before the campaign ended. Kennedy maintained his lead over Nixon. On November 9th he went on to win the election by a narrow margin. Four days after winning he said, 'It was the TV more than anything else that turned the tide.'

"Kennedy turned out to be one of America's most respected leaders. His presidency was cut short by an assassin's bullet in 1963 in Dallas, Texas. Nixon ultimately became president in 1968. He resigned in disgrace in 1974 after the *Watergate* scandal broke. Perhaps the viewers had it right. In any case, television was the game changer in 1960. Politics hasn't been the same since."

• • •

Evening was approaching. Paul said, "Dinner should be arriving soon. We don't eat it in the mess hall."

"That's probably a good thing," I responded. "Last time I ate in a mess hall I ended up in here." He laughed. "So, how do we eat?"

"They don't let us out as they do during breakfast," he said. "We eat it in our cells. They deliver food to us."

"Are you saying they only let us out once a day?" I inquired.

"Yes, once in the morning to eat and to clean up, that's it," he said.

Suddenly my stomach felt queasy, and then I felt aggravated. I'll be stuck in here for twenty-three hours a day, until I get out. Just thinking about it made me furious.

Paul said, "I need to put the books away before the guards show up."

I told him, "Go ahead. Do whatever you want. I'm in no mood to eat right now."

"I strongly recommend you eat," he said. "You can't order take out if you get hungry later." As Paul was putting away his books a deep feeling of hopelessness and despair settled over me. I felt like hanging myself. *Only if I had a savior*, I thought. *Only if someone could get me out of this prison.* I'd been depressed before, though never like this—almost to the point of crying.

Paul and I made idle chit chat for a while. We talked about our child-hoods, our likes and dislikes, things of the sort, but we didn't discuss American history. I wanted to tell him how terrible I felt, but I didn't have the guts. So we went on until supper arrived.

• • •

I heard the doorway down the hall open. Afterward I heard plates and flatware clanking together. It was dinnertime. A tiny slot on our door unlocked and a tray with two bowls on it came through. I said, "I thought the food in the low security wing was bad. This stuff is even worse."

"What did you expect, Filet Mignon?" Paul replied. "Acquiring decent food outside prison is difficult. What makes you think you're gonna get something appetizing in here? Dining in America is unpleasant. The food police assure that."

"I know, but for once I'd like to eat something that doesn't taste like wet cardboard," I told him.

He said, "Just eat. At least we're not starving." We both dug in. It was some sort of porridge. There wasn't anything tasty in it at all, or even

remotely flavorful. It was whatever they could scrounge up and mix together. Bland at best is how I would describe it. It was insipid like everything
else in the United States.

As Paul finished his meal I asked him if we could continue our
discussion.

He said, "Wait for the guards to come back. After they leave with our
bowls, we'll continue."

• • •

Minutes later they returned. We slipped our trays back through the
tiny slot on the door. They took them away and immediately left the wing.
As soon as they were gone I said, "We left off at television, and how it was
a game changer."

"That's right," Paul said. "Not only did TV change politics, it also
changed America. Right away, in 1950, concern over this new medium
emerged." He pulled out *Chronicle of America* and told me to read.

> 'If the television craze continues with the present level of pro-
> grams,' says Daniel Marsh, president of Boston University, 'we
> are destined to have a nation of morons.' A national survey shows
> children watch TV 27 hours a week, only 45 minutes less than
> their hours in school.[114]

"Mr. Marsh was correct. Eleven years later in 1961, this was said:"

> One youngster calls television 'chewing gum for the eyes' and the
> general mediocrity of the medium has prompted hard-hitting
> Newton N. Minow, 35, the New Frontier's chairman of the Federal
> Communications Commission, to put broadcasters on notice that
> station licenses won't be automatically renewed from now on. He
> says 'performance' will be judged against 'promises.' What does he
> think of present performances? 'A vast wasteland' of 'game shows,
> violence, formula comedies about totally unbelievable families,
> blood and thunder, mayhem, violence, sadism, murder . . . And
> most of all, boredom.[115]

"After 1961 it actually got worse. Early on, the 'boob tube,' as it was
known, was relatively tame. In the 1990s it became subversive, and in
many cases, downright perverted." I asked Paul if it caused the Revolution.
He told me, "It played a part! Without television, the American people
wouldn't have become materialistic and hedonistic so quickly. Television is
more than an entertainment device. It's a teacher. TV didn't create any new

standards and values, it disseminated them. Whoever controls the airwaves controls the culture, and whoever controls the culture, controls minds.

"There was oppression long before television. Despots have been around for millennia. Human beings haven't been safe since the dawn of civilization. Throughout our history it seems like somebody has been trying to put us all under a single yoke."

"Why do you think that is?" I asked.

Paul said, "For any number of reasons. Power is the main one." He brought up the Tower of Babel. I had heard of it, but, frankly, I never really understood it. He said, "Forty-three centuries ago in the land of Shinar, which is present day Iraq, human beings established the very first global empire. Back then the whole earth was of one language, and of one speech. It wasn't like it is today. A mighty hunter named Nimrod rose up and launched a kingdom called Babel." He told me to read from the *Bible*.

> And Cush begat Nimrod: he began to be a mighty one in the earth. He was a mighty hunter before the LORD: wherefore it is said, Even as Nimrod the mighty hunter before the LORD. And the beginning of his kingdom was Babel, and Erech, and Accad, and Calneh, in the land of Shinar. (Genesis 10:8–10 *KJV*)

"After settling down in a plain, Nimrod and his followers decided to build themselves a great tower. Read on," he said.

> And they said one to another, Go to, let us make brick, and burn them throughly. And they had brick for stone, and slime had they for morter. And they said, Go to, let us build us a city and a tower, whose top may reach unto heaven; and let us make us a name, lest we be scattered abroad upon the face of the whole earth. (Genesis 11:3–4 *KJV*)

"This lavish tower was to be the focal point of their civilization instead of God. Without it, everyone would've strayed from the flock. I guess you can say the Tower of Babel was mankind's first attempt at a new world order."

"Were they successful?" I asked.

"No," Paul answered. "God intervened and stopped the process. He saw what was happening and prevented its furtherance. Read on."

> And the LORD came down to see the city and the tower, which the children of men builded. And the LORD said, Behold, the people is one, and they have all one language; and this they begin to do:

and now nothing will be restrained from them, which they have imagined to do. Go to, let us go down, and there confound their language, that they may not understand one another's speech. So the LORD scattered them abroad from thence upon the face of all the earth: and they left off to build the city. (Genesis 11:5–8 *KJV*)

"God interceded. He erected language and cultural barriers to impede them, and He dispersed everyone across the planet. If those barriers weren't in place, and the people weren't separated, who knows what would've happened. Egyptian Pharaohs, Roman Emperors, Islamic Caliphs, British Monarchs, Soviet Marxists, and German Fuhrers all tried to do the same thing as Nimrod."

"And what's that?" I inquired.

"Unite the world under a single banner," Paul replied. "Babel was only the beginning. Unifying the human race under a single religious and political system has been the goal of despots for quite some time. Before television, that task proved difficult because of the hurdles God established and because of geography. After television came along, all that changed. TV made what was once impossible possible.

"Television and other mass media technologies, including the telephone, made the world a single community. The communication revolution that began in the 20th century provided autocrats something they hadn't had for forty-three centuries—the ability to speak to everyone on earth, all at once, at one single time. It made the entire planet the land of Shinar all over again.

"These modern machineries accomplished in a hundred years what no one else could do for more than four millennia. They bridged distances, which at one time were unbridgeable, and made the world a 'village' once again."

Then he said something I'll never forget. "The first step to changing the world is changing minds. Before good men follow, bad men fallow.[116] Like the Ten Commandments God gave Moses on Mount Sinai, new commandments like thou shalt have other gods before thee; thou shalt make unto thee graven images; thou shalt take the name of the Lord thy God in vain; forget the Sabbath day; dishonor thy father and thy mother; thou shalt kill; thou shalt commit adultery; thou shalt steal; thou shalt bear false witness against thy neighbor; and thou shalt covet thy neighbor's property came down from the airwaves into homes all across America, then into homes all over the world.

"The TV told us what to eat, how to dress, where to go, who was in and who was out, but it didn't say much as to why. It replaced parents and pastors as instructors. It became the focus of nearly everyone's attention. It was a unifying force—social engineers, advertisers, not to mention political forces, all knew it. They recognized they finally had a tool that could give them what they've always wanted—the devotion of the whole world.

"It's all about values, Tim. Whoever's values prevail, avail. And for the most part, the values that were seen on television were secular humanist values."

"What do you mean by secular humanist?" I asked.

"Secular humanists," Paul said, "are people who believe human interests and standards dominate. Basically, secular humanism is an atheistic or perhaps agnostic worldview that claims nature is all there is. Remember when I told you about scientism?"

I answered, "Yes."

Paul said, "Scientism rests upon it. It's a doctrine that automatically eliminates anything supernatural, or for that matter, dissent. Secular humanism is the ecumenical religion of our day—another *Tower of Babel*, so to speak. Remember, for something to be mainstream nowadays it has to stream mainly from secular humanism."

"Isn't that true?" I shouted.

He said, "Secular humanism monopolizes the West because secular humanists won't allow anything other than secular humanistic ideas in the public square. They replaced Judeo-Christian ethics, which helped shape Europe and America, and replaced them with their own naturalistic beliefs. Like sheep going to slaughter, Westerners did nothing because they thought they couldn't. Truth is, they could've, but didn't. They yielded to the tower. Now we're paying the price."

• • •

He said, "Around the same time television became popular, Christian ethics became taboo. In 1962 the United States Supreme Court, in an eight-to-one vote, ruled government-endorsed prayer in public schools was unconstitutional.[117] A year later in 1963 the Court ruled corporate reading of the *Bible* and recitation of the Lord's Prayer was also unlawful in public schools.[118]

"As society was being bombarded with wanton images in the 1950s and '60s, churches couldn't effectively respond. There was little anyone could do once the tower was set up. If anybody spoke out against secular humanism, they were either labeled crazy or a lawbreaker. Thus, very quickly, America went from being a Christian nation to a humanistic one."

He asked, "Before the Revolution, what do you think Americans cared about most?"

I told him, "Survival."

"No, that's now," he said.

"Food and shelter," I answered.

"Well, basic needs are essential, that's true. Tim, what was the center of their day to day lives?"

"I give up. Please tell me."

Paul said, "Amusement, diversions. Do you know what diversions do?"

I said, "No."

"Diversions divert attentions away from subversions.[119] Status was everything before the Revolution. See for yourself."

> It's open season on Americans. Readers have already been lambasted for being 'other-directed' (David Reisman) and materialistic (John Kenneth Galbraith). Now, it seems, they are also hung up on what the neighbors think.[120]

"Keeping up with the Joneses was more important than keeping God's commandments. Before the Revolution it was all about instant gratification. Getting mattered more than giving."

I thought *How could a television set do that?* It didn't make any sense to me. I asked Paul to explain.

He said, "Television, along with the federal government, forced Christianity out of public life. That, in turn, left a vacuum. The vacuum had to be filled with something and was. It was filled with materialism. Essentially, Darwinism supplanted Christianity as America's prevailing religion."

I asked, "How?"

He said, "Advancement of oneself over others became the norm. Altruism was abandoned and was replaced with egotism. The perception after television was, unless you're rich and famous, you're nothing. Hence, fame and fortune became the ultimate goal.

"People with the most were mostly looked up to. Pretenders became more important than achievers. Actors who played doctors and police officers were more successful than actual doctors and police officers.

Americans became fixated on celebrity. Their obsession with the wealthy and well to do became vice. Ultimately, it became their downfall."

• • •

I had heard the 1950s was an idyllic period. My grandmother told me it was a great time to be an American. I was confused. I asked Paul, "If our demise began in the 1950s, why are so many people nostalgic for that era?"

"It was a great period, don't get me wrong," he said. "I'd rather live then than now. The 1950s was a pleasant decade, indeed. However, it wasn't a great time for everyone. There were groups of people left behind."

CHAPTER 6

The Great Society

It is hard to lobby against
those who lob money.

THE SUN HAD SET. It was night again in the high security wing. Paul and I continued our conversation. He said after World War II, life was good for many Americans. He went on to say, "Still, getting ahead was difficult for some people. Blacks didn't have the same opportunities whites had, particularly in the South. Although slavery ended a century earlier, there was segregation."

"Segregation? What's that?"

He said, "Sorry. You never heard of it?"

"No."

"Segregation was a policy enacted after Reconstruction. Remember Reconstruction? We discussed it earlier," Paul asked.

I told him, "I remember. You don't need to explain it again."

He said, "Okay. Segregation began in 1877 after the federal government withdrew its forces from Southern territories. In the early 20th century it became entrenched in the Deep South and in border regions as a broad social policy. Segregation made black people second class citizens. They couldn't attend schools with whites, eat with them in restaurants, or even ride together with them on buses. Needless to say, blacks during this period were disadvantaged. For 88 years they were held back by the system." I asked did anyone help.

He said, "No, not really. America's new bourgeois class didn't care. As long as life was good in the burbs, the plight of the less fortunate living in ghettos didn't matter much to them."

I asked him, "Was anything done?"

He said, "Yeah. In the mid-1960s riots erupted."

• • •

"1964 was the beginning of the turbulent sixties," Paul said as he grabbed *Chronicle of America*. He started thumbing through it. "Pax Americana was over that year. The peaceful era between 1946 and 1963 that many Americans had enjoyed came to an abrupt end. Read for yourself."

> Riots in the state of New York have led to over 1,000 arrests, six deaths and the wounding of hundreds . . . These riots constitute the first serious racially motivated mob violence in a Northern state since the 1940s.[121]

"Rioting continued," he said. Then he grabbed the enormous book from my hand. "There's more!" he insisted. He found additional pages. Then he told me to read some more.

> Racial violence erupted again in Atlanta, where militant young Negroes shouting 'Black Power' attacked cars and police vehicles with chunks of concrete last night.[122]

> The worst race riot in the nation's history has ended here, leaving 38 people dead and sections of the city in charred ruins after four days of terror . . . Forty have been hit in the past week alone. Since the July rioting in Newark, New Jersey, racial strife has erupted in some 70 cities, including Atlanta, Boston, Philadelphia, Birmingham, New York and Cincinnati.[123]

He said, "Riots were a regular occurrence." I asked him why. He told me, "People take until they can take no more taking.[124] They burn who have nowhere to turn.[125] All gets obliterated when pressures are not mitigated."[126]

I said, "If we were to riot, government forces would annihilate us with their guns."

"Times were different back then," he replied. "Deadly force wasn't used the way it is now. Civil unrest got the attention of the feds, however. Instead of shooting bullets at protesters, Uncle Sam threw money at them."

"What do you mean by that?" I asked.

He said, "In 1964 the second nail was driven in liberty's coffin. What was meant to help did more harm than good."

• • •

"President Lyndon Johnson of Texas in 1964 went further than FDR," Paul said. "He asked Congress for 962 million dollars to fight poverty. In his first State of the Union Address he told legislators, 'Unfortunately, many Americans live on the outskirts of hope—some because of their poverty, and some because of their color, and all too many because of both.'[127] The following year he delivered another State of the Union Address. He asked Congress for federal support again. Read."

> President Johnson outlined his domestic aims tonight in his State of the Union address, calling for the creation of a 'Great Society' . . . Like the New Deal and Fair Deal before it, the Great Society is designed to help the politically and economically impoverished. It is founded on the premise that poverty and racial strife beleaguer the whole nation . . . He asked federal support for urban renewal, health care, education and the basic needs of the poor.[128]

"The *Great Society* was a social revolution unlike the *New Deal*, which was a governmental action. It was more like Woodrow Wilson's 1912 *New Freedom* platform.[129] The *Great Society* and *New Freedom* were crusades against inequality. They were federal efforts to expand economic opportunity to people at the bottom rung of society. Roosevelt's New Deal was more Keynesian. Its focus was ending the *Great Depression.*

"With help from the most liberal congress since 1938, Johnson passed into law all sorts of new programs including *War on Poverty, Medicare & Medicaid, National Endowment for the Arts and the Humanities, Jobs Corps,* and *Head Start.* In 1963 Johnson said, 'We have talked long enough in this country about equal rights. It is time now to write the next chapter—and to write it in the book of the law.'"[130]

"What's wrong with that?" I replied.

"Please hear me out," Paul said. "Johnson's goal was noble. His methodology was bad, however. Social justice justifies socialism.[131] Not everything he did was bad though. There were parts of the *Great Society* that were actually good. For example, Johnson signed into law many civil rights bills. Dwight Eisenhower, a Republican was the last president to do that."

I asked, "Did I hear you right? Did you just say Republicans pushed for civil rights?"

"They did," he replied. "Eisenhower signed the *Civil Rights Act of 1957*. It was the first piece of civil rights legislation passed in the United States since 1875. It established the Civil Rights Section of the Justice Department, which empowered federal prosecutors to obtain court injunctions against interference with the right to vote. The Civil Rights Commission had authority to investigate discriminatory conditions and recommend corrective measures.

"Republicans weren't the only ones who were calling for civil rights. Democrat John F. Kennedy sent National Guard troopers to Mississippi and to Alabama to accompany black students admitted to all white universities. He announced that he would send civil rights legislation to Congress. Ironically, he voted against Eisenhower's Civil Rights Act of 1957. In 1960 when he ran for president, he did an about face. He started making speeches supporting civil rights for blacks.

"Their civil rights agendas didn't go very far in Congress. There wasn't enough support for them among Congressional Democrats. Johnson was able to get things done, however. He signed the *Civil Rights Act of 1964*, the *Urban Mass Transportation Act*, the *Economic Opportunity Act*, the *Voting Rights Act of 1965*, the *Immigration and Nationality Act of 1965*, the *Higher Education Act*, the *Department of Housing and Urban Development Act*, and the *Demonstration Cities and Metropolitan Development Act of 1966*, not to mention 218 other pieces of legislation. By the end of his term, Congress had implemented 226 of his 252 legislative requests."

I asked, "Then what's the problem?"

"The *Great Society* had unintended consequences," Paul replied. "Good intentions have bad results."[132]

"Could you be more specific?" I asked.

"Okay," he answered. "For one thing, there's a lasting needy class in America because of the *Great Society*. Another thing it did is it ballooned the US budget." He pulled out a report containing United States Census Bureau statistics[133] and handed it to me. "Look here," he said. "In 1964 when the *Great Society* began, nineteen percent of Americans lived in poverty. In 1970 it was 12.6 percent." I looked at the report, the numbers were startling. According to the article, in 1980 the poverty rate was 13 percent. Ten years later in 1990 it was 13.5 percent. At the turn of the century in 2000 it was 11.3 percent. Thirteen years later in 2013 it was 14.5 percent. Paul was right. The stats were clear. The poverty rate didn't change that much during a half century. The only appreciable change occurred between 1964 and

1970. From 1970 to 2000, it changed very little, only 1.3 percent. After 2000 it started climbing again.

I said, "I guess the *Great Society* wasn't that great after all."

"Indeed," Paul replied. "In terms of its effectiveness, it was a dud. Johnson's War on Poverty produced very little. Its cost on the other hand was astronomical." I asked him how much did it cost. He said, "It's hard to say for sure exactly how much it cost. Experts estimate for the first fifty years it cost taxpayers 22 trillion dollars. That's trillion with a 'T.' The cost hasn't subsided either. That means we may never fully know its entire price. What we do know is federal and state welfare spending increased more than sixteen fold between 1964 and 2011."[134]

He asked, "Do you know what creates poverty?"

I told him, "Lack of money of course."

"No," he said. "Lack of money isn't the cause. It's lack of opportunity and lack of means. There's an underlying factor that produces poverty. Do you have any idea what it is?"

I said, "No, I don't."

"It's a broken family!" he shouted. "Families are society's bedrock. Good families make good citizens, and good citizens make good civilizations. More children were born out of wedlock after 1964 than ever before." He gave me another report. "Look here," he said. I grabbed the report and began to read. This report was just as eye opening as the other. In it there was a chart. I could clearly see in the mid-1960s the percentage of children born out of wedlock began to skyrocket. I could also see before 1970 less than ten percent of children born in the United States were born out of wedlock. By 2008 that number increased to 40.6 percent.[135] There was a clear correlation.

"Amazing," he said. "There's more." He flipped to another section and handed the report back to me. As I read farther I saw in the report more people born into poverty were born to single parents than to married couples.[136] I also saw unwed birth rates varied by race, and that blacks had the highest unwed birth rate.[137] I was unaware because nowadays just about everyone is poor, including whites, and hardly anyone is married. It took a report from the past to help me see why we had no future.

"Poverty wasn't eradicated," Paul said, "despite Johnson's effort. He perpetuated it." I asked him what he meant. He said, "Johnson, by trying to help poor people, helped even more people to become poor. The *Great*

Society didn't work. The reason being—single parent households became normal."

• • •

Government incentivizing poverty? That was new to me. What I heard was government saves us, and we all need largess to survive. And that if government didn't help, we'd all die in the streets. I heard all the benefits we enjoy in life, nobody built them. Each one of them is from government. This got me thinking. *Is any of that true? Or is Paul correct? Does government in fact impede our progress?* I asked him, "Please, tell me more."

He said, "Johnson wanted to help. He wanted to help minorities in particular. Right? Well, his welfare programs had the opposite effect."

I said, "Go on."

"Welfare works like this," he said. "Single mothers get money from Washington. When they have more kids they receive more money. If they make money, they get fewer benefits. If they have a husband, his income is added to hers, and she gets even less. Because of welfare, mothers remain in poverty and fathers remain apart from their children. Johnson didn't free anyone. He bound us to government. The dependent are always deficient.[138] Reliant men are compliant men."[139]

Paul did acknowledge something needed to be done, but, "welfare wasn't the answer," he said. "Welfare doesn't provide opportunity. It provides money. Free money is free from responsibility.[140] Instead of giving poor people money, Johnson should've given them a chance. Able bodied people need opportunities. They need to be able to provide for themselves and for their families. They don't need handouts. Entitlements enlist enslavements, and handouts hand out subjugation.[141] Johnson's welfare program had little effect on the poverty rate! If welfare mitigated poverty, why is everyone in America poor? We're all on welfare now!"

He had a point. Most of us were on public assistance. No one I'd ever known was self-sufficient. He was right. I asked, "Why is that?"

He said, "The practice of giving money out of the goodness of your heart to someone in need is called charity, and the practice of government taking money from your pocket out of duress and giving it to someone who will not work is called larceny.[142] Welfare is wealth redistribution. There's less money in the economy for consumers and for businesses when bureaucrats waste it and there's less economic activity and fewer jobs. Fewer jobs mean more people have to be on welfare. When unemployment remains high because it's impossible to find work, welfare becomes intergenerational."

I said, "So what! That doesn't explain anything."

"Let me finish," he said. "We live in a tyranny. You agree with that?" I told him I did.

He said, "In the past poor people didn't have a choice. They had to vote for progressive candidates in every election. Their livelihoods depended on it. Big government was the only option they had. I don't know if you've noticed," he said, "but New Socialists are the only game in town. They do whatever they want because they can. They have no opposition. We're boxed in because freedom was out boxed. Keep in mind, much poverty precedes much tyranny.[143] Epidemic flaps worsen whenever economic gaps widen."[144]

• • •

He said, "There was another seismic shift in the 1960s."

I looked at him, "What are you talking about?"

He replied, "The release of the pill."

I asked, "What pill?"

"The birth control pill," he answered.

I told him, "Let me see that!"

> The Food and Drug Administration today approved the use of a contraceptive pill. The hormonal tablets, which are said to be nearly 100 percent effective in preventing pregnancy, were tested over several years by women in Puerto Rico under Planned Parenthood supervision . . . Mrs. Margaret Sanger, the life-long advocate of birth control, is reportedly quite pleased with the news.[145]

I immediately scoffed. "Paul, how did a pill change America?"

"Simple," he answered. "It changed the male female relationship. The pill made people commodities, especially women. Sex became a recreational function instead of a relational one. After the pill was released, getting pleasure became more important than giving pleasure to someone. You see, Tim, when two lovers give, they each receive.[146] Men and women lose contact with each other when they become loose with each other.[147] The pill put distance between men and women."

I started laughing. "Paul, you're a prude. You're living in the past. Besides, what you just said is preposterous." As soon as I regained my composure I said, "What's wrong with sex? It's a lot of fun, you know."

"Absolutely nothing," he replied. "Sex is a gift from God. It sustains us. It gives us progeny. Not only is it fun," he announced, "we also need it to survive." He got my attention again. "Sex, is to be enjoyed. It's best when it's between a loving husband and wife. Its proper place is within a committed relationship. Otherwise, it's destructive."

"Destructive! How's it destructive?" I said with a chuckle.

He said, "Please, let me explain. The problem isn't sex. It's objectification."

I said, "I don't understand."

He told me, "Objectification of the body leads to desecration of the mind.[148] The pill started the *Sexual Revolution*, and the *Sexual Revolution* revolutionized man's evolution toward despair.[149] Sexual freedom brings carnal slavery.[150] Anything easy to get gets easy to let.[151] Lust and rust break down integrity.[152]

"Promiscuity hurts children. Loose parents loosen evil.[153] Broken adults beget broken children, and foul parents foul their offspring."[154]

I could relate to that. My parents weren't there for me. My father wasn't around. My mother Eunice, bless her heart, was overwhelmed. She had four children. Each one was from a different father. My parents' neglect prompted government parenting. My siblings and I struggled. We were reared by our grandmother Lois. The government paid her to rear us. We attended state-run schools set up for troubled youths. There we were taught everything.

When my grandmother stopped receiving checks from Washington she stopped caring for me. At age eighteen I was on my own. I turned to crime because I had nowhere else to go. I started robbing cars and burglarizing homes. Then I started mugging people. I didn't like doing it, but I had to eat. The whole time I was stealing I thought, *There has to be a better way*. If someone would've offered me something better, I would've taken it in heartbeat. Unfortunately, nobody gave me a chance. All I could do was steal. I couldn't even turn to my own parents for help. The world was a conundrum. Everywhere I looked there were obstacles.

Paul continued. "Uncommitted parents affect their children. Marriage benefits children," he said. I thought *I wouldn't know. My parents aren't married*. Evidently, all they wanted was a night of bliss. They didn't want eighteen years of responsibility. Apparently, they loved indulgence more than they loved me. He straightened me out.

I told him, "You're right, we get gratification from sex. We also get children. Who we have sex with is very important. People get pleasure from sex. Children get cheated when their parents aren't committed. I hadn't considered that. Thank you for bringing that to my attention."

He asked, "You want to know how the birth control pill changed America? By moving sex outside marriage!"

I said, "Then it's a tough pill to swallow. I can attest."

• • •

"About the pill," he said, "you don't know the half of it. The pill made Margaret Sanger's dream a reality."

I asked, "Who's Margaret Sanger?"

"She's the founder of *Planned Parenthood*," Paul replied. "Before her organization was called *Planned Parenthood* it was called the *American Birth Control League*. Margaret Sanger was a eugenicist."

"A eugenicist?" I commented. "What on earth is that?"

He answered, "A eugenicist is a student or advocate of eugenics. I know," he said, "you probably want to know what's eugenics. Before you ask, I'll tell you. The term eugenics comes from the Greek roots for 'good' and 'generation' or 'origin.' Eugenics has been around for a long time, at least since the time of Plato. It's a science that deals with the improvement of hereditary qualities of a race or breed. In essence, it's the self-direction of human evolution.

"In 1883 Darwin's half-cousin Sir Francis Galton coined the term eugenics. After reading his cousin's theories on evolution, he concluded desirable traits were inborn. Galton's ideas drew support in places like Germany, Great Britain, and in France for more than a half-century. They gained acceptance in the United States as well. One American who shared Galton's viewpoint was Sanger. She was a proponent of eugenics.

"Sanger opened the first birth control clinic in the US. She was an early feminist and women's rights activist. That's what they say. Truth be told, she was a radical socialist and a racist to boot. Margaret Sanger wrote and distributed a small newspaper called *The Woman Rebel* and circulated the pamphlet *Family Limitation*. She made the assertion 'a woman's body belongs to herself alone.'[155] In 1926 she spoke at a Ku Klux Klan rally in Silver Lake, New Jersey about birth control. And with aide from some influential black ministers, she initiated the *Negro Project* in 1939, which sought to significantly reduce the black population. Now, does that sound like a commendable person to you?"

I told him, "Not really."

"Many still do," he said with a look of disbelief. "The common thread of all eugenics is that all eugenicists hate commoners.[156] About birth control Sanger said this:"

> Eugenics without birth control seemed to me a house built upon sands . . . The eugenicists wanted to shift the birth-control emphasis from less children for the poor to more children for the rich. We went back of that and sought to stop the multiplication of the unfit.[157]

"The unfit get in the way. The strong need to eliminate the weak. Sanger's worldview was a lot like Darwin's. Remember when I told you about the Holocaust? Remember when I said eugenics is Darwinism's 'natural end?'"

I answered, "You did. I remember."

"Good," he said. "The six million who died in Hitler's Holocaust, do you think they're the only ones who are dead because of eugenics? They're not."

I said, "What do you mean?"

Paul said, "The contraceptive mentality led to abortion, and abortion, well, to put it blunt, the number killed by abortion is astronomical. It's in the untold millions. The body count is still mounting. Abortion became legal in the United States in 1973. The Supreme Court sided 7–2 with Jane Roe in the famous *Roe v. Wade* case.[158] That landmark decision made the killing of unborn babies a constitutional right. The Supreme Court did more harm to innocent life than Sanger ever did. She pushed for contraception. In her opinion, she thought abortion was an evil practice. She was opposed to abortion. In 1932 she wrote:"

> Although abortion may be resorted to in order to save the life of the mother, the practice of it merely for limitation of offspring is dangerous and vicious.[159]

"All of a sudden seventy-five years ago, because of a judicial decision, unborn babies lost the most fundamental right—the right to life."

"Okay, that's enough." I announced. "I don't want to hear anymore! None of this matters. Who cares about a bunch of cells?"

"You should!" he shouted. "Abortion isn't like contraception. Contraception kills potential new life. Abortion kills life at its earliest most vulnerable stage. Sacrificing the unborn for the born, saving the strong at the weak's expense is what abortion is all about. Those cells deserve the same dignity we all deserve. Unborn babies are alive. They meet the same seven criteria for life every other living thing does. Yes, they're composed of cells. They have different levels of organization. They use energy. They respond to their environment. They grow and they adapt to their environment. Down the road they reproduce. Everyone is the same. We're small initially. Then we grow to adulthood. Time, Tim! Time is the only difference! It's what distinguishes an unborn child from a full grown adult!

"Why should we be concerned, you ask. This is why. If you give somebody the right to murder someone, you've given everybody the right to murder everyone." I could see the grief in his eyes.

He didn't say a word. I said, "Paul are you all right?" He was quiet.

A few seconds later he said, "It continued."

"What continued?" I asked.

"The eugenics movement," he said. "It continued." He paused again. "At first abortion was voluntary. Most abortion clinics were located in large metropolitan areas particularly where there were large minority communities. More nonwhite babies were aborted per capita than white babies. In 2011 thirty-seven percent of abortions were performed on black babies.[160] Black people only made up twelve to thirteen percent of the population. Fast forward to 2048. Every major hospital in America is required to have an abortion wing. There's a de facto forced abortion policy in place here in this country. Women are being nudged."

I said. "Are you saying they have no 'choice?'"

He answered, "They're being blackmailed. Government is withholding welfare from poor women. That is, if they don't terminate their pregnancies. By deciding who gets aid government is deciding who lives and dies. Everything Margaret Sanger wished for is happening today. Rich elites are the only ones reproducing!"

I screamed, "Okay! Please stop! I can't believe what I'm hearing. Government is bad, I can see that, but it isn't evil."

"This government is. There's more," he said. "If forced abortion was the only thing happening, that would be bad enough. Unfortunately, euthanasia is widespread."

I said, "Euthanasia, come on. It's voluntary. My grandmother was euthanized. She told me she wanted to die. Euthanasia is an act of mercy."

"Is it?" he asked. "In 1994 when Oregon voters passed Measure 16,[161] legislators from that state used the term 'assisted suicide' instead of euthanasia. After 1994 other states followed suit passing their own right to die measures, also calling the practice 'assisted suicide.' The term assisted suicide is an oxymoron. Suicide is the act of taking one's own life. If someone assists in another person's death, the term suicide doesn't apply. The term homicide is more appropriate. As we speak, assisted suicide is legal in all fifty states. Everyone in America has access to it, similar to abortion, and like abortion government forces it on the poor."

"All right, that's it!" I interrupted. "I won't hear another word. My grandmother wasn't murdered, if that's what you're trying to say. She wanted to die," I repeated.

"I know this is difficult," Paul said. "Was she poor?"

With tears streaming down my face I answered, "Yes."

He asked, "When she died, what happened to her? What did the doctors say?"

I started sobbing. "They said they didn't have the resources—she needed to be transferred to another facility. She was in great agony. Weeks went by. The doctors did nothing. They said, 'Her condition requires a specialist.' She finally decided to die. She told me she could no long endure the pain."

Paul grabbed my shoulders. "Believe me. She didn't want to die. Your grandmother is dead because the hospital couldn't save her. She was poor, and so was the hospital. They didn't transfer her to a different facility because of the backlog. She was low on the list. She didn't make the cut. When socialists promised us free healthcare, they sold us a bill of goods. Communists promise freedom before they dispense enslavement.[162] Healthcare is rationed. It's all part of eugenics."

He asked, "What ailment did she have?"

I told him, "It was respiratory disease. Her lungs were full of fluid."

He said, "Was it treatable?"

I told him I didn't know. I said, "I'm not a doctor. Before she finally died she lived three weeks in the hospital. I don't know anything else."

He asked, "Where was she admitted?"

I said, "In a government run hospital—the geriatric wing I believe. Why?"

"Now don't get upset," he said. "Geriatric wings are where bureaucrats send old people to die." He handed me a 2033 report from The Department of Health and Human Services. Inside the report were these words: "The Hippocratic Oath needs to be eliminated to cut costs . . . life-saving care can simply be denied to the elderly and costs will be saved." He said, "There's no way to treat everyone. They can't afford it. Every procedure isn't covered. If you offer sex change operations to the young and strong, the old and feeble are going to be denied. It's a matter of economics. There's only so much largess to go around. The American health care system is a triage. They didn't murder your grandmother. She was disposed of. Before that she was deprived."

My grandmother was everything to me. I loved her so much. When I heard she had died because she was old and because a cold bureaucracy refused to give her adequate care that was too much for me to bear. I instantly lost control. "If I ever get out of here, I'm going kill them!" I rushed to Paul's secret chamber. "Do you have any books in here on how to escape from prison? I want to avenge my grandma!"

He said, "Please, be quiet. The guards are down the hall. Calm down. Listen to me. This is why human cells need our consideration. Abortion devalues human life. Abortion was the initial step. It's been widely accepted since 1973 that unborn babies are disposable. Now old people are expendable. Parents have been killing their children in abortion clinics for decades. Now those parents are being killed in hospitals without their children knowing it.

"Where are we because of abortion? Let me tell you. All over the world things are out of whack because of it. The demographic imbalances we see today are largely the result of abortion. Many babies have been aborted in the West. Western countries are now in steep decline. Most people living in the West are over sixty-five. The number of young people is shrinking at an alarming rate. In China and in India there's a great gender imbalance. In those countries there're more boys than girls because girls are selectively culled. Normally there's a 50/50 ratio if the population isn't tampered with. Eugenicists thought there'd be too many people. They miscalculated. Truth be told, there're too few people. At least that's the case in the developed world. Most industrialized nations can't even maintain their own populations. The 2.33 children per woman requirement needed to retain a stable populace isn't being met. Human body parts are sold openly on the market to researchers and to doctors for profit without any remorse, as if they're a commodity. Who'd thought that seventy-five years ago?

"Problem is we think we know better than God. We think we can improve His creation." Paul opened the *Bible*.

> There is a way which seemeth right unto a man, but the end thereof are the ways of death. (Proverbs 14:12 *KJV*)

"Commandments are not there to resist, but to assist."[163] he explained. "If we had listened to God, we wouldn't be in this mess."

• • •

It felt like a truck had just hit me. Paul came over. "It's sickening, isn't it?"

I told him, "I don't want to hear any more. It's not like we can do anything. I'll just lie here and die. Please, leave me alone."

He said, "That's what the socialists want. They want us to give up."

I asked, "What can we do?"

He said, "We can be informed. There's more. Please, listen."

I responded, "What else is there?"

He said, "I'm only half-way done. There's more you need to hear. I need to tell you about the 1960s counterculture movement. It changed America more than anything else." He grabbed *Chronicle of America*.

> 'We want the world, and we want it now,' thundered Doors lead singer Jim Morrison this year . . . The San Francisco 'Summer of Love' began, more or less, in June at the Monterey Pop Festival. With the Beatles' masterpiece, *Sgt. Pepper's Lonely Hearts Club Band* as a beacon, the feeling that rock music had come into its own merged with a high-flying counterculture movement.[164]

"The Summer of 1967 was a pivotal time in American history. That's when the so-called *Age of Aquarius* began. Times were already changing." He flipped to another page and pointed.

> 'Be-bop-a-lu-la, she's my baby' may have been poetry enough for an earlier generation of music fans, but as Bob Dylan sings on his new album, *The Times They Are a Changin'.*[165]

"The *Age of Aquarius* wasn't anything new. It resembled ancient Greece and ancient Rome. The *Bible* describes the Pre-Christian pagan world this way." He read some passages from the Good Book.

> Ye know that ye were Gentiles, carried away unto these dumb idols, even as ye were led. (1 Corinthians 12:2 *KJV*)

> This I say therefore, and testify in the Lord, that ye henceforth walk not as other Gentiles walk, in the vanity of their mind, Having the understanding darkened, being alienated from the life of God through the ignorance that is in them, because of the blindness of their heart: Who being past feeling have given themselves over unto lasciviousness, to work all uncleanness with greediness. (Ephesians 4:17–19 *KJV*)

"Decadence is as old as time. So is idolatry. Before Gentiles received the Gospel in the first century A.D. they, too, worshipped the creature more than the Creator." He said, "Look here."

> Because that, when they knew God, they glorified him not as God, neither were thankful; but became vain in their imaginations, and their foolish heart was darkened. Professing themselves to be wise, they became fools, And changed the glory of the uncorruptible God into an image made like to corruptible man, and to birds, and fourfooted beasts, and creeping things. Wherefore God also gave them up to uncleanness through the lusts of their own hearts, to dishonour their own bodies between themselves: Who changed the truth of God into a lie, and worshipped and served the creature more than the Creator, who is blessed for ever. Amen. (Romans 1:21–25 *KJV*)

"A new age was ushered in. That's true. Young activists generated confusion instead of peace. They created an era of hedonism. Read this," he said.

> To parents surveying the times through horn-rimmed glasses, the world of youth may look confusing. Colleges, which have doubled enrollment since 1960, are breeding a new hedonism.[166]

"That's when we lost our moral foundation. We lost it in the mid-1960s." He handed me a report. It was from Gallup, a polling firm out of Washington, D.C.

"A poll?" I replied.

"Just read it," he said. The number of people who said religion was 'very important in their life' fell sharply in 1964.[167] He handed me another report. I saw the crime rate started skyrocketing around the same time.[168]

"There's a correlation," he said.

I told him, "I can see that. What happened in 1964? Why was it a turning point?"

"You ever heard of nihilism?" he asked.

I replied, "No, what's that?"

"It's a doctrine that denies any objective ground of truth and especially of moral truths. Nihilists reject all religious and moral principles. They believe traditional values and beliefs are unfounded and that existence is senseless and useless," he answered.

I asked, "Where did the idea start?"

"It originally came from Russia." Paul said. "There it was identified with a loosely organized revolutionary movement that rejected the authority of the state, church, and family. Radical professors in America took the idea and ran with it. They started teaching it to students in the 1960s."

"It made its way in through education?" I asked.

"Yeah," he said. "Abraham Lincoln the sixteenth president of the United States is attributed as saying, 'The philosophy of the school room in one generation will be the philosophy of government in the next.' Vladimir Lenin the Russian communist leader and revolutionary and head of the Soviet Union from 1922 to 1924 is claimed to have said something similar. It is widely believed he stated, 'Give me four years to teach the children and the seed I have sown will never be uprooted.' These two statements from these two very different men make the same point."

"Which is?" I asked.

"That changed people change nations.[169] That if you want a revolution, you don't need an army, all you need is curriculum," he replied.

He was right. There was an established orthodoxy in the public school system. When I was attending school we all knew it was best to keep our mouths shut and to tow the line. We understood words could get us in a lot of trouble. In particular I remembered one classmate in 2043. He had the audacity to question the teacher. He said, "The Revolution was a mistake." She called him a menace and threw him out of the classroom, and then she told the rest of the class he was dangerous. Everybody was stunned. I told Paul, "Maybe you're right."

He said, "I am. Hijacked schools turn out instructed tools.[170] When education becomes indoctrination, the schooled get fooled.[171] The education system is a great vehicle. Radicals know that. They've been exploiting it for quite some time. They've been turning students into useful idiots for a long time now. Remember, Tim, people controlled by their lusts are easy to control, and weak believers are easily swayed by strong deceivers.[172] They are readily played whose minds are easily swayed.[173] Minds consoled by socialists are controlled by socialists."

I replied, "I agree, but I have to ask, did students really take over America?"

He said, "Before socialism can dominate, it must germinate. It has to take root before it takes over. Men become cattle before they become chattel. Those students eventually grew up. The counterculture movement was a society of detached young hippies. Later on it became a political force present throughout the land." He told me to read from *Chronicle of America*.

> Two new tracts are spreading the gospel of the New Left. Theodore Roszak takes an academic slant in *The Making of a Counterculture*. Scorning science and reason ('the myth of objective consciousness'), he laments 'the final consolidation of a technocratic totalitarianism in which we shall find ourselves ingeniously adapted to an existence wholly estranged from anything that has ever made the life of man an interesting adventure.' The only antidote is a 'standard of truth' pegged to 'illuminated personality.' Roszak's plan pales beside the visionary ramblings of Jerry Rubin, Chicago Seven defendant and cofounder, with Abbie Hoffman, of the Yippies. In *Do It*, Rubin predicts a 'Youth International Revolution,' staged by 'tribes of long hairs, armed women, workers, peasants and students.' The White House is slated to 'become one big commune.'[174]

"The best way to penetrate is to infiltrate. Infiltration is a lot easier than confrontation.[175] Socialists learned that early on. They got into more than just education. They got into politics. Their plan backfired, however. Efforts to usher in the *Age of Aquarius*, which was supposed to be about universal brotherhood rooted in reason, ended up rekindling old hostilities with reason itself being at the center of it all."

CHAPTER 7

The Second Civil War

Freedom from reality ends up
being enslavement to futility.

I WAS TIRED. I told Paul, "Let's get some sleep."

He said, "Before we turn out the lights, do you want to know how the second civil war got started?"

I said, "Sure. Tell me."

"The first shots of the second civil war were fired August 29, 1968 at the Democratic Convention in Chicago, Illinois."

"Who shot at whom?" I asked.

He said, "It wasn't a shooting war. It was ideological. Read for yourself."

> A splintered Democratic Party nominated Hubert Humphrey as its presidential candidate on the first ballot tonight. Humphrey defeated Senator Eugene McCarthy by more than 1,100 votes, but the party he will lead against Richard M. Nixon is far from united . . . Faced with anarchy in the party, Humphrey turned to Edmund Muskie of Main, as a quiet friend in the Senate, as his running mate. In his acceptance address, Humphrey urged his party to look to the future. 'If there is one lesson that we should have learned, it is that the politics of tomorrow need not be limited by the policies of yesterday,' he said.[176]

"Chicago was marred by violence, protests, and mayhem during the convention. Scores of demonstrators and police officers were injured. It wasn't a conventional war, however. This was the beginning of what we know as the 'Culture War.' After the convention, the exodus began."

I asked, "Exodus? What exodus?"

Paul said, "The exodus of conservatives from the Democrat Party to the Republican Party. Remember when I said, 'Many in the South switched their allegiance to the Republican Party?' That began in 1968. Southerners were more conservative. In 1968 they started moving to the GOP." I asked him why.

He told me, "Leftists crashed the Democrat Party. A schism emerged during the convention. Control of the South started shifting that year because of party infighting.

"The Democrat Party wasn't always a leftwing party. Martin Van Buren, who subscribed to the political theories of Thomas Jefferson and a coalition of Jeffersonian Republicans, formed it in the 1830s from Jefferson's Democratic-Republican Party, which fell apart in 1824. The Democrat and Republican parties were both inspired by Thomas Jefferson. They had many similarities despite their differences. At least it was that way until 1968." I asked him what changed.

He said, "It was the counterculture movement. Democrats started becoming Republicans in 1968, and Republicans, well, according to Democrats, they became fundamentalists. The 1960s were the 1860s all over again."

After those words I fell asleep.

• • •

I had an amazing dream that night. I saw a man unlike any other. He had limitless power and a kingdom that wasn't of this world.

I saw one of His closest friends had betrayed Him, then His own had brought Him before a counsel—it was a trial. He looked like a Lamb heading for slaughter. The men who held Him were mocking Him and beating Him. I was amazed. He didn't say a word. He had the ability to stop them, but He didn't. He allowed the abuse.

This man was an enigma. The entire world was against Him. Yet, He was the only man in the world without sin. His accusers were vehement. They yelled, "Blasphemer!" before they called for His death. I saw Him take a guilty man's place. Then He was led outside the city where He was to die. They kept beating and mocking Him along the way. With the weight of the world bearing down on His shoulders He kept moving forward. He was obedient unto death.

They hung Him between two criminals. The entire world could see Him there. "He isn't going to reign over us," everyone shouted. "We've broken the cord. We're victorious," the world screamed. Death was His target. Life was His purpose. I saw Him die on a hill that night. Then I saw death die with Him.

The man's name was Freedom. I saw prison doors open when He died. Then I saw the captives let out. Upon His death the dead were made alive. I heard another man say, "By condemning the Just Man this one time, the condemned are now justified forever. You're free now because He freely gave Himself."

• • •

I woke the next morning. I didn't tell Paul about the dream, mainly because it didn't make any sense. I didn't say a word. I just got ready for breakfast. "Make sure there're no documents lying around," Paul said.

I told him, "Right," then I waited for the guards to show up. I couldn't stop thinking about the dream.

He said, "After breakfast I'll tell you more about the second civil war."

"Sounds like a plan," I replied. I had had many dreams before. There was something different about this one. It was vivid. It was a message.

Suddenly, I heard a sound. It was the door opening down the hall. I said, "The guards are coming."

Paul reacted, "We're good." I couldn't wait to get out. The cell walls were closing in on me. When I heard the sound of dangling keys a feeling of relief came over me. I prepared for the guards to enter.

One yelled, "Get back," then the cell door opened. "You know the drill!" the other shouted. Paul and I got on the floor. They restrained us, and then we were led out. One guard grabbed me and the other grabbed Paul. We walked down the hallway shoulder to shoulder toward the shower. As we were walking it reminded me of the dream. I just knew there was something to this dream. I didn't know what.

After showering we ate. It was the same garbage we had had the night before, a porridge of some sort. It tasted as bad as I had remembered: awful. I said to Paul, "If I have to eat this every day, I want the death penalty." He laughed. The guards looked at us. They knew what we were talking about. After we were done with our breakfast, the guards restrained us again, then they marched us to our cell, where we were in isolation again. The dream came to mind along the way. *Who was this man, and why did He die?* I wondered if I'd ever get an answer.

The moment we got back, the cell door closed behind us. Paul said, "The Democrats controlled the South for thirty-six years. After Franklin Roosevelt was elected, Dixie was called the Solid South until Democrats lost control in 1968."

"That's politics!" I exclaimed. "What about the second civil war? On with it!"

"Be patient," he said. "The point I'm trying to make is both civil wars began in the South. That's the only similarity though."

I told him, "Okay. Go on."

He said, "The first civil war began in 1860. It started when South Carolina succeeded from the Union and it was over in 1865 once Robert E. Lee surrendered his forces to Ulysses S. Grant at Appomattox Courthouse, Virginia. The second civil war is quite different. For one thing it isn't over. For another, it's a clash of worldviews. It's a battle for hearts and minds. Whether or not the federal government has the right to regulate or even abolish slavery within an individual state isn't the issue anymore. The central issue now is truth, whether or not it's slavery, and if we're free to determine it for ourselves."

I was reminded of the dream. There was a clash. It was between the man and the world. I was about to say something. I decided to remain silent instead. "What's truth?" Paul asked. "Can we know it? To some people the answer is simple. God is truth, and, yes, we can know it. To others it's an anathema. They won't touch it because of its implications."

"I'm not following," I remarked.

He replied, "Truth is avoided because it cannot be voided.[177] Truth has moral consequences, particularly when truth points to God. God is at the center of the Culture War. Morality hinges upon God, specifically on whether or not He exists."

I said, "Morality? What exactly is morality?"

"I'm glad you asked," he replied. "If God exists, morality is God's very nature. If He doesn't exist, morality is whatever we say it is. It's either absolute, or it's relative. There's no in-between. Have you heard of relativism?"

"No," I answered.

"It's a theory," he said. "It's a belief that knowledge is relative to the limited nature of the mind and the conditions of knowing, that ethical truths depend on the individuals and groups holding them. It's a post-modern idea iconoclasts embrace. Libertines love it because it justifies wanton behavior. Whether we want to admit it or not, we all live by moral standards—it just depends on whose standard we apply.[178] The Culture War is a contest between competing values. Whose morality applies is at stake. The counterculture movement was antiestablishment. Free love and recreational drug use were its hallmarks. Eastern philosophy was its foundation. It was at odds with Christianity. Its values were contrary to biblical values."

I asked, "In what way?"

He answered, "Biblical values are absolute. They come from God. Counterculture values on the other hand are subjective. They come from within. There's no way to mix the two."

"Wait a minute," I responded. "What do you mean they come from within?"

He said, "Timothy Leary, the 1960s counterculture guru and psychologist, coined the term Reality Tunnel, a phrase derived from Aristotle's Representative Realism. His friend and associate, Robert Anton Wilson, popularized the Reality Tunnel idea writing, 'All that we know is what registers on our brains, so what you perceive (your individual reality-tunnel) is made up of nothing but thoughts.'"[179] "They come from within because according to Leary and Wilson truth isn't objective."

I said, "That's what I was taught. Truth isn't the same for everyone. What's true for you may not be true for someone else."

He said, "There is nothing more untrue than everything is true.[180] The absolute statement 'there are no absolutes' is absolute malarkey. People who do not acknowledge real truth acknowledge themselves real fools.[181] Truth is actual. It's ideal. You cannot battle truth.[182] Relativists cannot stand truth because it stands in their way.[183] That which is right is difficult to fight."[184] He asked, "How do you make repulsive behavior acceptable?"

I replied, "I don't know. How do you?"

He told me, "You make it incontestable. The hippy lifestyle was controversial. Americans found it reprehensible. To some it was sinister. It wasn't the kind of thing most Americans were used to—to them it was an Eastern cult. New Agers knew they couldn't win America over if the old biblical standard remained. They needed a new standard, so they looked to an English magician and self-avowed new age prophet for another law—the law of Thelema was the answer.

"They adopted the old edict 'do as thou wilt, for this shall be the whole of the law.' Aleister Crowley's rewritten early 20th century occult law was largely forgotten for decades until hedonists made it their mantra. The popular rock band The Beatles even put Crowley on the cover of their *Sgt. Pepper's Lonely Hearts Club Band* album. The law of Thelema mandates each person follow his or her True Will to attain fulfillment in life. It also prohibits anyone from interfering with any other person's True Will. It's a form of moral relativism because it eschews ethical standards and because it places morality in the hands of individuals. It's a new yardstick . . . one that let's everyone decide for himself what is right and wrong.

Unlike the Judeo-Christian standard, which is absolute, it's a belief that no standpoint is uniquely privileged over any other. It's a means to an end. It means to end all truth. It's a way to cut religious cords."

I remembered the world shouting, "We've broken the cord." Everyone was rejoicing. Was this a clue? All the sudden the dream started making sense. The man was the center of conflict. The world hated Him. It wanted Him gone. It attacked Him, yet He couldn't be destroyed. I began to think *Why is this man so hated, only if I knew.*

Paul saw I wasn't paying attention. "Tim, are you listening?"

I replied, "Sorry, please continue."

He said, "After the high bar is removed, every low bar becomes just as valid as any other.[185] Friction is a function of opposing forces.[186] Groups at odds cannot be in league.[187] People who never agree always agree to part.[188] The law of Thelema was the beginning of the Revolution."

I said, "How did it start the Revolution?"

He answered, "It removed the one thing that was holding Americans together."

"And what's that," I replied.

"Judeo-Christian principles," he answered.

Out of the blue I had an epiphany. It never dawned on me before—why America was so cold. The answer was simple—everybody does their own thing. Nobody looks out for anyone else. There's no cohesion in this nation. Paul explaining the law of Thelema helped me understand why that is.

I thanked him for his insight. After responding with a thank you of his own he said, "Common ways pave the way for peace.[189] Here's the standard rule, peaceful rule is uncommon without a common standard. The Confederates in an attempt to keep slavery split the Union in 1860. They failed in the end and the US was still united. In an effort to free America from its

Judeo-Christian foundation the counterculture movement united the new left. It was successful. America is now divided. Its goal was freedom. Its end was tyranny. The crusade for peace and love caused division and strife before it spawned the Revolution."

• • •

"Eventually the 1960s gave way to the 1970s. Nevertheless, Americans were still divided over the Vietnam conflict and other hot button issues like the environment and social problems. Even though Woodstock was over the Culture War was still in full swing. Read here," Paul said.

> The radical way of life of the late 1960s seems to be turning into the mainstream attitude of the early 70s . . . A lot of people are like Archie Bunker of TV's *All in the Family*, nostalgic for the days when we didn't have a welfare state and a meathead for a son-in-law.[190]

"Despite this, according to Richard Nixon there was still a 'silent majority' in the United States. He coined the term on November 3, 1969 during a nationally televised speech when he called on them for support saying, 'And so tonight—to you, the great silent majority of my fellow Americans—I ask for your support.'[191]

"Remember Nixon?" He asked. "He's the guy who ran against Kennedy in 1960 and lost. I already mentioned him. Anyway, he won the presidency in 1968. He beat Hubert Humphrey to become the 37th president of the United States.

"Richard Milhous Nixon was a US congressman and senator from California before he was president. He was vice president under Dwight D. Eisenhower from 1953 until 1961. Nixon was a polarizing figure. His anti-communist reputation made him popular with Republicans. Democrats abhorred him because he expanded the Vietnam War into Laos and Cambodia. Despite reneging on his campaign promise to reduce US troop levels in Vietnam he was reelected in 1972. He beat George McGovern in every state except in Massachusetts and the District of Columbia. Almost every state in the Union supported him. Nixon was riding on high in 1972. A year later in 1973 his fortune changed after the *Watergate* scandal broke."

"Water what?" I asked.

"The Watergate office complex in Washington, D.C., where the Democratic National Committee was headquartered," Paul replied. "It was broken into on June 17, 1972. Five men who were paid by Nixon aids were responsible. The break-in triggered a congressional investigation. Congress discovered Nixon had been abusing his federal power. Facing certain impeachment he resigned in disgrace on August 9, 1974. Sixty-nine other people were eventually indicted and twenty-five were convicted. To make matters worse Gerald Ford gave him a full pardon. President Ford's pardon had a polarizing effect.

"In 1976 the tide turned against Republicans. Ford had marred himself by pardoning Nixon two years earlier. In 1976 when he ran for a second term he lost to a relative newcomer named Jimmy Carter.

"The former one term Georgia Governor ran an effective campaign. He ran as a reformer. He beat the incumbent president on November 2, 1976 to become the 39th Commander in Chief."

I asked Paul, "Was he successful?"

He said, "Not exactly. Carter didn't fare any better than Ford. He was seen as weak. While he was president, interest rates soared, so did unemployment. There was an energy crisis, long lines appeared at gas stations, and many feared another oil shortage like the one in 1973. Carter had different foreign policy ideas as well. He believed the United States should employ its military to intervene as little as possible and that American military power should be used scarcely. He preferred the US take the lead in promoting universal human rights instead.

"In 1979 he looked particularly weak. Fifty-two American diplomats were taken hostage in Tehran that year, a month later the Soviet Union invaded Afghanistan. America was at a low point. In 1980 the tide turned again. This time the momentum shifted back to Republicans."

I asked Paul, "What happened?"

He said, "Ronald Reagan was swept into the White House. It was a historic landslide victory. In 1981 during his inauguration speech he urged the nation to 'begin an era of national renewal.' He claimed, 'Government is not the solution to our problem, government is the problem.'[192]

"He was re-elected in 1984. It was another landslide victory. The economy began rebounding in the 1980s. There was strong economic growth for about eight years. Reagan rebuilt the nation's struggling military making it the most lethal fighting force the world had ever seen, but not everyone was satisfied."

I said, "What do you mean?"

"His presidency was tarnished by *Iran Contra*, unprecedented deficits, and increased income inequality, not to mention, President Reagan's policies drove liberals crazy. He was a simpleton in their eyes," Paul said. "He was the embodiment of the crude religious right, and as it is now, back then, a rift existed between traditional right wing conservatives and progressive secular liberals. Regardless, conservatives including Democrats supported him. He was able to galvanize them into a substantial political force—there's a remnant of that force that still exists today. The coalition he formed changed politics forever. Reagan supporters weren't all the same, yet they did have one thing in common."

"And what's that?" I asked.

He said, "They thought America was on the wrong track, and they wanted a strong nation again. The most notable members of the Reagan coalition were the evangelical Christians. Religious conservatives turned off by crime, social disarray, and abortion were particularly disillusioned. They started mobilizing in 1979, two years before Reagan became president. Please, read," he implored me.

> The Rev. Jerry Falwell held a revival meeting on the steps of the New Jersey State House today. Or was it a political rally? Falwell, who reaches an audience of 18 million with his television ministry, founded the Moral Majority two years ago to spread the church's conservative agenda.[193]

"Falwell's Moral Majority helped Reagan beat Carter, who himself was an evangelical. Reagan Democrats were the key to Reagan's two lopsided victories. Social conservatives within the Democratic Party, many of whom had never voted Republican in the past pulled the lever for Reagan two presidential election cycles in a row. It was all because of his social conservatism and his hawkishness.

"There was a silent majority after all as Nixon had said. Reagan demonstrated that in 1980 and again in 1984. The religious right was an asset for the GOP. The coalition Reagan built in 1980 helped Republicans again in 1988. After Reagan's second term was over, George Bush was elected. He became president on November 8, 1988. He wasn't as conservative as Reagan, notwithstanding, he governed for the most part as the former president had. Liberals were unhappy for another four years. Lucky for them in 1992, the tide turned yet again."

I said, "I got to hear this!"

Paul told me, "A bad economy and Bush's inability to end it helped Arkansas Governor Bill Clinton. He was the first Democrat elected president in twelve years. He was elected on November 4th with forty-three percent of the popular vote and 370 electoral votes. Clinton said he was a 'New Democrat,' fiscally responsible, yet socially liberal. He was the opposite of Reagan. He was the right's boogeyman."

I asked, "Was that the end of the religious right?"

"No," Paul replied, "In 1994 they struck back. Fueled by dissent over abortion, gay rights, gun control, and other issues, social conservatives supported the Republicans again, shifting the electoral balance against the Democrats. Consequently, Republicans retook Capitol Hill. Read here."

> Republicans won control of both houses of Congress, for the first time in 40 years, in yesterday's elections. In the Senate, 53 of the 100 seats are now Republican, and in the House there are now 230 Republicans and 204 Democrats. Voters turned out Democratic governors as well, including New York's Mario Cuomo, defeated by George Pataki; a majority of the statehouses are now Republican. Republicans say the results are a rebuke by voters to Bill Clinton, who said today, 'They sent us a clear message—I got it.'[194]

"I guess that was the end of Clinton," I remarked.

He said, "It wasn't. After he lost Congress he retooled himself. President Clinton and the Republican Congress achieved a budget surplus through the years 1998 and 2001 by scaling back the welfare state, something not seen since 1969, and like with Reagan, there was considerable economic growth and peace during his tenure as president. He was a very successful Commander in Chief. On November 5, 1996 he was reelected.

"Here's the thing," he said, "despite his achievements, Americans were still divided. The US was a 50/50 nation. There's no better illustration of this than the 2000 presidential campaign between George W. Bush and Vice President Al Gore."

I replied, "You said George Bush was elected in 1988."

Paul laughed. "No, not that Bush, his son. George W. Bush ran against Clinton's veep. The result was tighter than anyone expected. Gore won the popular vote: 48.4 percent supported him, and 47.9 percent supported Bush. Bush won the presidency however. He received 271 electoral votes. Gore only got 266.

"The election was very close. It took thirty-five days to declare Bush the winner. What's more, the Supreme Court was involved. It decided to end the recounts in Florida on December 12, 2000. Bush won that state by 537 votes. His victory in 2000 came down to fewer than a thousand votes. Talk about a squeaker! In 2001 he went on to become president. Less than a year later the United States was attacked."

CHAPTER 8

Fundamental Transformation

Only go to war if the result of not fighting
is worse than the result of fighting.

I KNEW WHAT HE was talking about. I said, "You mean 9/11."

He responded, "You know about it?"

I said, "Yes. Islamic terrorists flew two planes into the World Trade Center buildings in New York City and one into the Pentagon. Another plane went down in Pennsylvania. It was the worst attack on American soil since Pearl Harbor."

"I'm glad you're aware," he replied. "Do you know what happened after 9/11?"

I knew less about its aftermath. My grandmother was in New York City that day visiting relatives. She said everyone was terrified; nobody knew what to do. I heard about 9/11 when I was a child. It was the kind of thing that was sacrosanct. Hardly anyone talked about it in detail. The attacks changed America. I understood that, still no one explained how. Looking at Paul I could see there was more to the story. His gaze was revealing.

• • •

"The nation was caught off-guard. The attack was like the October 29th, 1929 stock market crash. Government grew again because of the assault. Bush like Franklin Roosevelt asked Congress for more power. He spoke at the FBI Academy in Quantico, Virginia. There he said, 'For the sake of the American people, Congress should change the law and give law enforcement officials the same tools they have to fight terror that they have to fight other crime.'[195] Congress had already passed legislation. Forty-five days after the terrorist attacks, the House passed the *Patriot Act*. Two days later on October 26, 2001 it became law. Republicans and Democrats were united. The measure passed 357 to 66 in the House. In the Senate it passed 98 to 1."

"That's great!" I yelled. "Democrats and Republicans were unified!"

"Wait a minute," he said, "there's more. Civil liberties groups were concerned."

"About what?" I asked.

"According to them, parts of the law violated the fourth amendment. Government could spy on ordinary Americans. That was their argument," he said.

I told him, "Could you be more specific?"

"Sure," he replied. "The *Patriot Act* gave the US Department of Justice and other federal agencies new powers on domestic and international surveillance of electronic communications. Congress removed legal barriers that once blocked law enforcement, intelligence, and defense agencies from sharing information about potential terrorist threats and coordinating efforts to respond to them."

I said, "What's the big deal? The Government spies on us all the time."

He told me, "Things were different fifty years ago. America doesn't have a bill of rights anymore. Back then it did. Nowadays nobody cares. In the past it wasn't that way. The American people still had fire in their belly. Unlike today, there was something to preserve. Liberty still existed."

I asked him, "What are you saying?"

He answered, "There was another threat to freedom besides terrorism. Unchecked government posed an even bigger danger. The *Patriot Act* was an antiterrorism measure designed to prevent another 9/11 style attack. It was supposed to keep Americans safe. Problem is it was a precedent. Many of its provisions set the stage for a future takeover."

• • •

I said, "It was the *Patriot Act*!"

"Not entirely," Paul reacted.

I said, "What's that supposed to mean?"

His answer came without delay. "The *Patriot Act* was superseded by the *USA Freedom Act* in 2015. Two days after controversial provisions of the *Patriot Act* expired, Congress passed another antiterrorism bill. It's gone. It's not the law of the land anymore. Socialists took away our freedoms. It wasn't the *Patriot Act*. It gave them the tools however."

I looked at him. "Oh."

He said, "Although data mining of Americans' phone calls and information was specifically prohibited by the *Patriot Act*, huge data centers designed to support the Intelligence Community's efforts to monitor, strengthen, and protect the nation were set up in 2011. Those data centers put us at risk. They stored all forms of communication including private emails, cell phone calls, and Internet searches—parking receipts, travel itineraries, bookstore purchases, and other digital pocket litter was also kept. Exabytes of information were warehoused at these facilities.

"The problem with the law was its potential for abuse. The NSA after 9/11 as part of President Bush's war on terror established the *Terrorist Surveillance Program* to intercept Al Qaeda communications overseas. The program gave government the ability to monitor without warrants the communications of people inside the US with suspected connections to Al Qaeda. Whistleblowers claimed the agency's goal was 'to create a database of every call ever made.' All of this was done without a warrant or any judicial oversight. Informers maintained the NSA could then data mine and analyze this traffic for suspicious key words, patterns, and connections.[196]

"On August 17, 2006 a federal judge ruled Bush's warrantless wiretapping program was unconstitutional and ordered an immediate halt to it.[197] The Attorney General of the United States on January 17, 2007 announced to Congress the program wouldn't be reauthorized by the president. Six years later the American people learned it was replaced by a new NSA program.

"*Patriot Act* provisions were set to end on June 1, 2015. A day later Congress enacted the *USA Freedom Act*. The new law ended the controversial collection of bulk metadata. The legislation required the government to obtain a targeted warrant to collect phone metadata from telecommunications companies."

I asked him, "Why did you say 'many of its provisions set the stage for a future takeover?'"

He said, "Even though the *USA Freedom Act* modified several provisions of the *Patriot Act*, NSA computers remained at the carriers' and service providers' switching offices. The NSA continued taking both meta-data and content from phone records and text messages. The difference was they did it from another location. The technological infrastructure for collecting bulk metadata established in the wake of the 9/11 attack never dissipated. It's still around today.

"Don't get me wrong, the *Patriot Act* was a great law enforcement tool for fighting terrorism. The problem is the police aren't the only ones using bulk surveillance. Today it's being used by our government. It's used to control the economy. What's more, digital technology was used during the Revolution. Congress didn't anticipate the events of 2037."

I said, "What do you mean?"

"The digital framework Congress set up after 9/11, which could monitor US citizens was abused," Paul claimed. "Socialists began using the computer networks. That's how the American people were subdued!"

• • •

"Congress wasn't thinking in 2002 either," he said. "That year the House and the Senate passed a joint resolution—one that gave President Bush war-making powers. It was an authorization for war."[198]

I said, "Against whom?"

"The country was Iraq," Paul responded. "Intelligence sources within the Bush administration were convinced Iraq was in violation of several United Nations Security Council resolutions. Their main concern was that Saddam Hussein still had weapons of mass destruction. Bush went to the United Nations a year and a day after the 9/11 attack to present his case. He urged delegates there to compel Iraq to comply with Security Council directives on weapons of mass destruction saying, 'Our greatest fear is that terrorists will find a shortcut to their mad ambitions when an outlaw regime supplies them with the technologies to kill on a massive scale.'[199]

"He went there to build 'a coalition of the willing.' On November 8, 2002, the UN Security Council passed Resolution 1441 unanimously. The resolution gave Iraq final notice to cooperate with UN inspectors. Soon after his September 12th UN speech President Bush sought approval from Congress. On October the 11th he got it. The Iraq War Resolution passed the Senate that day. It voted 77 to 23 in favor of the measure. 'Authorization for Use of Military Force Against Iraq' was approved in the House 296 to 133 the day before. The bill was signed into law October 16th.

"Secretary of State Colin Powell was sent to the UN a year later. On February 5, 2003 on behalf of the Bush administration he appeared before the United Nations Security Council. There he made this statement:"

> Last November 8, this council passed resolution 1441 by a unanimous vote. The purpose of that resolution was to disarm Iraq of its weapons of mass destruction. Iraq had already been found guilty of material breach of its obligations, stretching back over 16 previous resolutions and 12 years.[200]

"Powell's visit had cleared the way for the Iraq War. A month after his speech on March 20, 2003 Iraq was invaded. Forty eight nations joined Bush's 'coalition of the willing' in what the US called 'Operation Iraqi Freedom'. At first there was broad support for the war—seventy two percent of the American public according to Gallup favored military action.[201] Congress was also on board. Bush's approval rating hit 71 percent March 30.[202] On April 9th Saddam Hussein had disappeared, and Iraqis were jubilant.

"The campaign was going well at the beginning. Within three weeks, coalition forces captured Baghdad, soon after, the Baath Party fell. Saddam Hussein went on the run shortly thereafter. The first month of the war was a success. On April 14th victory was declared. A couple weeks later on May 1st the president atop the USS Abraham Lincoln announced an end to major combat operations."

I said, "The war was short?"

"Hold on," Paul replied. "There's more. Insurgent fighters started pouring into Iraq. The war was far from over. May 1st wasn't the end. It was the beginning."

I said, "What do you mean?"

"Overthrowing Saddam Hussein was the easy part. The hard part," he said, "was keeping the peace. Saddam Hussein was the only thing holding Iraq together. Iraq's population was diverse. Shia Arabs lived in the south. They made up half of Iraq's population. Sunni Arabs lived in the country's center. They comprised about a quarter of the people, and Sunni Kurds who lived in the north were a somewhat smaller share at around fifteen percent. Toppling Saddam's regime altered the balance of power.

"With Hussein gone the situation in Iraq quickly deteriorated. Sectarian violence broke out in every Iraqi city where there was a mixed population. Sunni and Shiite militias took over neighborhoods and drove out residents of the opposite sect. At the heart of the struggle was the ongoing fight for power in the region."

"Slow down," I begged. "I'm not following."

"Saddam Hussein crushed everyone who opposed him," he said. "Sunni Arabs installed by British colonialists as proxy rulers in the early 20th century managed to hold onto power after Iraq was granted independence. Disbanding the Iraqi army and purging members of Saddam's ruling Baath Party from government ignited a Sunni led insurgency. American soldiers fighting in Iraq found themselves in the midst of a civil war, one dating back centuries. To make matters worse coalition armies were the primary target of insurgents. Homegrown militia groups and foreign fighters opposed to the American led occupation used asymmetric warfare and a war of attrition against American forces and the American supported Iraqi government while conducting coercive tactics against rivals or other militias.

"Do you know the worst part?" he asked. "Turns out Bush's intelligence sources were wrong. There were no weapons of mass destruction in Iraq! UN and US inspectors working in Iraq searched nearly 1700 sites for two years. They concluded Saddam Hussein destroyed his WMDs. Hans Blix who oversaw the UN investigation 'described the evidence Secretary of State Colin Powell presented to the UN Security Council in February 2003 as shaky.'"[203]

• • •

"The Iraq War was a colossal mistake," Paul said. "It cost taxpayers almost two trillion dollars. The human cost was even more. Over four thousand US servicemen and women lost their lives during the campaign. It was all for naught."

"All for naught?" I replied.

"Yeah, Iraq ended up a failed state. Speaking of mistakes," he said, "let me tell you about the housing bubble. It all started with the 'Ownership Society.' The president wanted everyone in America to own his or her own home." He pulled out a copy of one of Bush's speeches from his secret chamber and told me to read.

> This Administration will constantly strive to promote an ownership society in America. We want more people owning their own home. It is in our national interest that more people own their own home. After all, if you own your own home, you have a vital stake in the future of our country.[204]

"The Housing market was already strong in 2003. The Dot-com bubble had collapsed in March of 2000."

I said, "So what!"

"Let me continue," he responded. "The NASDAQ hit an all-time high on March 10, 2000. The next day technology shares started falling. Falling stock prices prompted a real estate boom. In January 2001 as a result of the Dot-com collapse, the Fed started lowering interest rates. On January third the interest rate for borrowing money dropped a half point to six percent. It was the first rate decrease since late 1998. The Fed kept lowering interest rates. By August that same year the rate which banks charge each other on overnight loans of their reserves was cut almost in half to three-and-a-half percent. After 9/11 policy makers cut the rate in half again. Interest rates kept falling. Eventually they were lowered to just one percent in June of 2003.

"Money was cheap and plentiful. Plunging interest rates reduced the cost of owning a home. Cheaper money meant lower mortgage payments, and lower payments meant more people could afford expensive homes."

I asked him, "What's wrong with that?"

"Nothing," he said, "if lenders were betting on borrowers instead of the rising home values."

I told him, "You lost me again."

He said, "Rising home prices were built into mortgages and into mortgage-backed securities. The housing market was a Ponzi scheme. It was based on an assumption that overtime home prices would keep climbing, and that people would pay their mortgages on time like they did in the past. The problem was people weren't buying homes as they had in the past. They were buying them for short-term selling rather than for long-term dwelling. Many people were looking at their houses not as homes but as investments they could flip overnight for a hefty profit."

I asked, "Did anyone try to stop it?"

"Are you kidding me?" he said. "Wall Street was euphoric. It was making money hand over fist. Banks were bundling loans together into mortgage-backed securities and reselling them to investors around the world. Their bets were paying off. Other people behind them were buying them out by placing bigger bets, and others behind them were raising the bidding even higher. Investors weren't concerned either because rating agencies gave the securities AAA ratings. Their modeling showed even risky subprime loans were performing well."

I told him, "That sounds like madness."

"It was," he commented. "The biggest reason for increased borrowing was interest-only and no-money-down loans. The housing market was hot. It was so hot almost anyone could get a loan. Congress relaxed the underwriting standards for mortgages in 1977."

I asked, "How did they do that?"

He said, "In a bid to encourage depository institutions 'to help meet the credit needs of the local communities in which they are chartered' Congress passed *The Community Reinvestment Act*.[205] The law was enacted to urge commercial banks and savings associations to help low and moderate income neighborhoods and to prevent what's called redlining. It established a regulatory regime for monitoring the level of lending, investments, and services in traditionally underserved communities.

"Examiners from federal agencies assessed and graded lending institution's activities in low and moderate income neighborhoods. If a regulatory agency found out a lending institution wasn't serving these neighborhoods, it could delay or deny that institution's request to merge with another lender or to open a branch or expand any of its other services.

"CRA regulations were revised as part of the Clinton administration's initiative to create performance-based and objective standards. The new regulations attempted to satisfy community activists by focusing more attention on the lending, investment, and service records of banks. The regulations also attempted to reduce the amount of paperwork required of lending institutions.

"Needless to say unscrupulous lenders took advantage of the law. Mortgages companies stopped asking their clients for paystubs or tax returns."

I asked, "Why would they do that?"

He said, "Because they didn't care—it didn't matter to them whether or not someone could pay off their loan. It was irrelevant. Institutions chartered by Congress, particularly Fannie Mae and Freddie Mack were buying up their mortgages, guaranteeing their repayment, bundling them into securities, and reselling them to investors.

"More mortgages meant higher home prices and more speculative activity. Home prices were climbing faster than household incomes. Spending on housing was taking up a bigger and bigger share of people's earnings. Consequently, consumers became dangerously overextended. They didn't have enough money left over for other things. It was just a matter of time before something gave.

"On July 10, 2007 something gave. The financial system started crumbling. That's when Moody's Investment Service and Standard & Poor's admitted they blew it. Standard & Poor's, the American financial services company axed 612 different bond issues worth 8.3 billion dollars. Moody's did the same to 399 securities with a face value of 5.2 billion. Never before had those agencies downgraded so many bonds. Even though less than one percent of the securities backed by junk mortgages were affected, the downgrades set off a chain reaction that quickly spread throughout the world. By the first week of August liquidity started evaporating and the markets began seizing up. By the second week banks were afraid. Lending took a dive, and investors were afraid. They wouldn't even refinance short-term commercial debt, which had nothing to do with mortgages. By the third week in August hedge funds and private equity firms were getting squeezed.

"Thirteen months later in 2008 Wall Street fell into complete disarray. On September 15th Leman Brothers collapsed after the Treasury and the Fed declined to rescue it. Merrill Lynch looked like it was going to fail as well until it sold itself to Bank of America. The economy went into seizure mode. Top policy makers in Washington quickly jumped in. On September 18th, Treasury Secretary Hank Paulson proposed the biggest taxpayer funded bailout in history. He recommended the government spend up to 700 billion dollars to buy up troubled assets.

"On September 29, 2008 after Paulson's plan was rejected by the US House of Representatives the stock market lost 777 points, or seven percent of its value. It was the biggest ever single-day crash in the market's history. The Dow lost 1.2 trillion dollars in market value that day. From there things got worse. On October 7th the Dow lost 508 points. Two days later it lost 678 points. On October 15th it plunged another 733 points. Finally, on October 22nd it was down another 514 points. By October the stock market crashed about forty percent from its 2008 high. Wall Street went into a freefall late in 2008 with no bottom in sight. It didn't learn."

"It didn't learn what?" I asked.

"It didn't learn from the 1929 stock market crash. Home prices were overvalued. Their appraisals were too high," Paul said. "Easy lending brought too many people into the market. Mortgage firms made big loans to people who couldn't pay them back. The American dream became the American scheme. Home ownership instead of being a delight became the fast track to poverty for many people. The rush to be rich only hastens scarcity, and scarcity, well; it's the road to uncertainty."

• • •

I said, "That's it! That's how we all ended up in slavery, isn't it? They ruined the economy . . . of course."

"Not exactly," Paul answered. "The Bush administration had to intervene."

I said, "What do you mean?"

He said, "Bush who said there'd be no bailouts did an about face. He asked Congress for standby authority to lend to companies unlimited amounts of money. Fannie Mae and Freddie Mack, remember them, they couldn't raise fresh capital. Paulson announced the government would take them over. He put them into a conservatorship and backed them with billions of dollars. Bush didn't let the market fix itself. He did like Herbert Hoover. His administration tried stimulating the economy.

"The Federal Reserve went on a money printing spree. Between September and the end of December, the Fed had created an extra one trillion dollars out of nothing. Its balance sheet ballooned from about 900 billion dollars to two trillion in less than four months. The Fed was frantically pumping money out through a host of new lending programs designed to jump start frozen credit markets.

"Toward the end of the Bush presidency, the Treasury and the Fed were trying to bail out the entire banking system. The government provided taxpayer money to hundreds of banks and a handful of insurers and automakers, including Citigroup, AIG, Fannie Mae, Freddie Mac, GM, Chrysler, and Bank of America as part of the 700 billion dollar *Troubled Asset Relief Program*, or TARP.[206] The Federal Reserve left the spigots on for a half-dozen lending programs. It bought up mortgage-backed securities in a bid to push down rates on home loans."

I asked, "Did it work?"

Paul said, "It depends on who you ask. Some argue 'TARP didn't save us from a Great Depression; instead, it nearly drove us into a Great Depression.'[207] Others claim TARP 'helped stabilize the economy, using only $410 billion of its authorized $700 billion.'[208] It's hard to say who's right. Nobody knows what would've happened had TARP not been passed. What the economy would've been like without TARP is anyone's guess. We'll never know.

"We do know that economic weakness persisted. Economic growth was only moderate averaging about two percent in the first four years of the recovery. The crash in the housing sector led not only to the financial crisis, it also caused a downturn in the broader economy. The unemployment rate doubled from less than five percent to ten percent. It was at historically high levels, particularly the rate of long term unemployment. Experts say the *Great Recession* lasted eighteen months. It was the longest lasting recession since World War II."

• • •

I said, "All this junk about banks and bailouts is beginning to bore me. I want to know how we ended up in slavery. Come on, Paul, just tell me."

"Be patient," he said. "I'm getting there. What happened next was the American people went to the polls in 2008 'hoping for change.' Republicans were reeling that year. Bush damaged his own party. All the turmoil his administration caused helped Democrats. On November 4th Republicans lost the presidency again. Barack Obama defeated John McCain to become the 44th president of the United States. Incidentally, Obama was the first black president ever elected. His presidency was historic. At first the nation was behind him, particularly the black community. Later on that 'changed.'"

I asked, "What happened?"

He said, "The same forces that the Bush administration was beholden to were also around during the Obama presidency. The *Great Recession* was over in June of 2009. Yet, in the face of prolonged weakness, the Federal Reserve maintained an exceptionally low level for the federal funds rate target and sought new ways to provide additional monetary accommodation. These included additional LSAP programs, known more popularly as quantitative easing, or QE."

"So you're saying Obama continued Bush's polices," I commented.

"Exactly," he replied. "By then it was too late. Wall Street was addicted to cheap money. In 2009 President Obama signed the *American Recovery and Reinvestment Act*.[209] The law was commonly referred to as The Stimulus Package. It sought to end the 2008 recession by spurring consumer spending and saving between 900,000 to 2.3 million jobs. It had three spending categories. It cut taxes by 288 billion dollars. It spent 224 billion dollars in extended unemployment benefits, education, and health care, and it tried to create jobs by allocating 275 billion dollars in federal contracts, grants, and loans."

I said, "Well, did any of it work?"

He told me, "Again, it depends on who you ask. Some people say it did. They maintain ARRA did better than planned. In one way they're right. By the end of fiscal year 2009, only 241.9 billion dollars of the 787 billion dollars allocated were actually spent. Yet, critics point out the plan didn't succeed because the economy contracted 2.8 percent. It was supposed to save 900,000 to 2.3 million jobs. As of October 30, 2009, it saved only 640,329 jobs. There's disagreement over the law like with TARP. It prevented a second recession many say. Others claim it was a boondoggle. Determining who's right is very difficult."

I asked, "Did anything change?"

He said, "Not really. Life in America was essentially the same with Obama as president. The market began to improve in 2009. On March 9th that year the Dow hit a twelve year low. Then it started to climb again. It kept climbing. In 2011 the market made a full recovery. In 2013 the Dow hit an all-time high. Wall Street did fine under President Obama. It was a different story on Main Street, however.

"The real estate boom wasn't over in 2008. Prices fell after the crash, but the cost of buying a home was still higher than it was before the boom. The situation actually got worse because neighborhoods which once offered less expensive housing were totally gentrified. Prices were still high because of low interest rates and because there were more wealthy people in the market.

"Rising markets and swelling real estate prices helped create nearly 500,000 new millionaires. After the number of millionaires in America plunged in 2008 the number of households worth five million dollars or more set a new record in 2014. There were 142,000 households worth twenty five million dollars or more in 2014, up from 132,000 in 2013. That year there were more than twice as many millionaire households in the US than there were in 1996.[210] If you look at the upsurge in housing prices starting in the late 1990s, it paralleled the explosion in the number of rich people living in the country. Fewer people were able to buy a place of their own because they were bidding against the largest most affluent class in American history.

"To make matters worse rent increases were a fact of life in many large US cities. Wealthier families produced a shrinking pool of moderately-priced rentals. Swelling rental populations brought growing demand. Developers mostly targeted the top of the income spectrum because it was more profitable. High rent was a particular problem in urban areas where the best jobs, or in some industries, the only jobs were located. Moving somewhere else where there was more affordable housing wasn't an option for many people because their job was located in a place that was doing well.

"A lot of people thought it was a great time for real estate because of the historic low rates. It's true that low interest rates helped some people buy homes. It's also true low interest rates have a downside."

"You're losing me," I interrupted. "What are interest rates?"

He looked at me. "Interest is the price of borrowing money. When savers want to lend out money they charge interest. Typically when interest rates are low, they're plenty of savers competing against one another. That wasn't the case when Obama was president. The Fed was printing money out of thin air to create the illusion of savings in the marketplace. They wanted to keep their debt payments low and avoid spending cuts. It all came at a cost."

"How's that?" I asked.

He peered at me again. "Inflation. Printing money out of thin air dilutes the value of the dollar. Prices climb as the buying power of the dollar falls."

I told him, "You lost me again."

"There was too much money chasing too few goods," he answered. "When demand grows faster than supply, you have price increases."

I thought back to our discussion about supply and demand. I said, "Oh yeah, supply and demand."

"Good, you remember," Paul answered back. "That was the case here. The price of goods and services rise as the cost of living increases, and when wages can't keep up with inflation, the standard of living decreases. This is what happened in the early twenty-first century. Inflation is a hidden tax that destroys savings. The Fed was pumping air into a massive bubble. If the Federal Reserve Bank wasn't involved, interest rates would've rose as people saved money instead of spent it. There would've been less money in the marketplace and the price of interest would've gone up as a result.

"The Fed was trying to maintain a healthy economy. It was spurring the economy by making corporate and consumer borrowing easier. It was taking whatever means it could to prevent significant deflation in the United States because consumers, businesses, and governments were in so much debt they could never pay it all back. Problem is when interest rates are artificially low, there's no reason to save. Saving is good. Savings create strong stable economies. Low interest rates provide very little return on savings. Low rates triggered by inflation are what make savings worthless. Most savers during times of inflation are losing monetary value instead of gaining it. And do you know who inflation affects the most?" Paul asked. I told him no.

He said, "Inflation hits the lower and middle classes especially hard. Higher food prices, surging fuel costs, increased rent, and utilities all mean there's less money available once these necessities are paid for, leaving little for savings or discretionary spending. Work-related costs such as transportation and child care, as well as other expenses like medical care and taxes drive more people into poverty.

"Nearly 5.5 million more Americans were living in poverty in 2013 than in 2008. The median household income declined 4.6 percent during Obama's first five years in office.[211] It was down three percent as of 2014. The official poverty rate was 1.6 percentage points higher.[212] Real median household income dropped more than 1000 dollars from 2009 to 2014, or 2.3 percent to 53,657 dollars.[213] It was the first time in US history Americans lost real income gains during an economic recovery. Obama's economy was particularly hard on those already at the bottom. From 2009 to 2014 the bottom fifth of households saw their average income fall by eight percent. In Obama's first year in office, 43.6 million people, or 14.3 percent of the population lived in poverty. By 2014, that number climbed by more than three million, pushing the poverty rate to 14.8 percent.[214]

"After the *Great Recession* the gap between the richest Americans and the rest of the country widened. Obama said, 'Our country cannot succeed when a shrinking few do very well and a growing many barely make it.'[215] For all of his talk about income inequality the stats clearly show his policies didn't help the middle class. His economic record ran contrary to his rhetoric. Income inequality was worse under Obama than George W. Bush."

• • •

Paul claimed, "The situation in the Middle East was even worse."

I asked, "In what way?"

He said, "Obama decided not to extend a 2008 Status of Forces Agreement[216] the Bush administration made with Iraqi Prime Minister Nouri al-Maliki that would've left ten thousand soldiers in Iraq. Obama promised if he was elected president, he would bring all US soldiers home. On

December 18, 2011 he made good on that promise. The remaining soldiers who were in Iraq left that day in accordance with the agreement. After the last convoy departed for home approximately one hundred soldiers were left behind."

I said, "So? That's a good thing, isn't it? Didn't you say the Iraq war was a mistake?"

"All hell broke loose!" he replied. "Iraq wasn't stable. Its security was still in question. The United States government screwed up in 2003! Bush's decision to invade Iraq was a blunder. Hardly anyone disagrees. Obama made another error in 2011. By withdrawing military forces too early. The retreat left the door open for terrorists. His eagerness to leave Iraq and his failure to leave a residual US force behind to support the Iraqi army abetted the rise of ISIS."

I asked, "What's ISIS?"

He answered, "Al-Qaeda in Iraq, better known as the Islamic State in Iraq and Syria. It was a terrorist army many thousands strong known for public beheadings and mass executions. Islamic militants from all over the world joined the group. It was formed in 2006 as a small insurgency and it grew fast because of all the US military equipment it was able to seize— equipment our government left behind after its departure.

"In 2009 ISIS began to shift its focus from Iraq where it was largely unsuccessful. In 2011 it set its sights on a whole new front - the civil war in Syria. It all began with the *Arab Spring*."

"The Arab what?" I reacted.

"The *Arab Spring*," he replied. "It was a series of anti-government democratic uprisings that arose independently and spread across the Middle East. Millions of people in the Arab world took to the streets in 2011 demanding dignity, democracy, and social justice. The movement began in Tunisia on December 17, 2010 after a 26-year-old man named Mohammed Bouazizi set himself on fire in front of a local municipal office because police confiscated his cart and beat him. The *Arab Spring* quickly spread to Egypt, Libya, Syria, Yemen, Bahrain, Saudi Arabia, and Jordan.

"In its wake Egyptian and Tunisian security structures, which kept Islamic extremists in check were disbanded. The movement backfired. Jihadis knew they could exploit the confusion and vacuum in power created by the unrest. Activism in Tunisia and in Egypt inspired nationwide protests in Syria. Pro-democracy demonstrations erupted in March of 2011 in the city of Deraa. Demonstrators took to the streets in protest against President Bashar al-Assad's regime."

I asked, "What did Assad do?"

"He met the protesters with a massive crackdown," Paul replied.

I asked him, "Then what happened?"

He said, "Opposition supporters who demanded Assad's resignation began to take up arms. After months of military sieges, the conflict gradually morphed from mass protests to an armed rebellion. Soon it was a full-blown civil war with at least a thousand different rebel groups participating. ISIS was one of the rebel groups. It took control of large swathes of Syria and Iraq.

"From Syria ISIS cut its way back into Iraq. The Iraqi military turned and ran in the face of the assault. Iraqi soldiers abandoned their weaponry, stripped off their uniforms, and fled. The challenge from ISIS proved too much for the newly formed army."

I asked, "Was Iraq under ISIS's control?"

"No," he said. "Iraqi government forces in Baghdad fought back. They stopped the ISIS advance. Though on the way to Baghdad ISIS was able to pick up support. It took numerous cities and towns as it went. It was especially ruthless in its targeting of minority groups in areas that came under its control. Age old communities were forced to flee their ancestral lands. The Christians and Yazidis suffered heavily under ISIS. Men, women, and children, Muslims, and Christians where all killed by ISIS. Fellow Sunni and Shia Muslims who didn't ascribe to its strict brand of Islam were also killed. The group destroyed priceless archaeological sites and took female unbelievers as slaves.

"Mosul, Iraq's second largest city was also captured, and so was Tikrit, Saddam Hussein's birthplace. Nevertheless, Iraqi forces managed to stop Islamic State militants from taking the ultimate prize, Iraq's capital city. Six months after Mosul fell, ISIS began to stall. That wasn't the end however. There was a refugee crisis, which affected Europe. Millions of Syrians and Iraqis were forced to flee their homeland. They ended up mostly in European countries. The Russians got involved in the conflict as well. Syria was the Soviet Union's ally during its cold war with the West. Syria hosted the only naval base Russia had in the Middle East at the port of Tartus on the Mediterranean Sea.

"Russia began bombing targets in Syria on Assad's behalf days after Russia's president Vladimir Putin outlined his position in a speech to the

United Nations General Assembly. The move prompted warnings of further bloodshed. The whole thing was a mess."

I said, "What did Obama do?"

He told me, "Next to nothing. Critics, especially in the GOP ranks, called for more aggressive US military action against ISIS, but Obama pushed back. On sending additional US soldiers to fight ISIS he said, 'It is not just my view, but the view of my closest military and civilian advisers, that that would be a mistake.'[217]

"ISIS leaders were hit with airstrikes by the United States and its coalition partners instead. Obama's approach was different than Bush's. Obama felt restraint was the better course of action. US and coalition air forces didn't want any civilian casualties. The focus on protecting civilians added a wrinkle to the bombing campaign. Pilots were already operating without help from spotters on the ground who could call in strikes on known ISIS targets. Obama believed killing innocent civilians would hand the extremists a major propaganda victory and alienate both the local Sunni tribesmen and Sunni Arab countries that were part of the US-led coalition.

"His strategy was to contain ISIS into increasingly restricted territory. He hoped the Islamic State would fail on its own, rather than because of the actions of a foreign power. Obama's tactics against ISIS were ineffective. Minimal airstrikes alone weren't enough to defeat the terrorists."

$$\bullet \; \bullet \; \bullet$$

"Foreign policy wasn't President Obama's strong suit. He was more interested in domestic issues. In 2008, about a week before he was elected, he said, 'We are five days away from fundamentally transforming the United States of America.'[218] On March 23, 2010 he did."

I asked, "What's so important about that date?"

Paul said, "That was the day President Obama signed the *Affordable Care Act*. That's when the medical industrial complex was born—you know the one that let your grandmother die. Today healthcare is provided by the state. Back then it wasn't. The *Affordable Care Act*, better known as Obamacare was the first step toward the awful government run healthcare system we know today. It wasn't properly vetted."

I said, "What do you mean?"

He said, "You don't know?"

I look at him. "No."

"It was rammed through Congress. Legislators didn't have time to read the massive 2700-page bill. Nancy Pelosi who was the Speaker of the House at the time said, 'We have to pass the bill so that you can find out what is in it, away from the fog of the controversy.'[219] Jonathan Gruber who helped craft the healthcare law suggested lawmakers and voters didn't know what was in the law or how it worked financially, and that's what helped it win approval." He pulled out an article where Gruber was quoted.

> You can't do it political, you just literally cannot do it. Transparent financing and also transparent spending. I mean, this bill was written in a tortured way to make sure CBO did not score the mandate as taxes. If CBO scored the mandate as taxes the bill dies. Okay? So it's written to do that . . . In terms of risk rated subsidies, if you had a law which said that healthy people are going to pay in, you made explicit healthy people pay in and sick people get money, it would not have passed. Lack of transparency is a huge political advantage. And basically, call it the stupidity of the American voter or whatever, but basically that was really really critical to get for the thing to pass. Look, I wish Mark was right that we could make it all transparent, but I'd rather have this law than not.[220]

"Democrats passed Obamacare using the temporary sixty-vote Senate supermajority they gained through a Minnesota recount and the prosecution of then Alaska Senator Ted Stevens. After they lost the 60th vote, they resorted to a dubious legislative procedure called Reconciliation. Senate Majority Leader Harry Reid cut a deal with Nancy Pelosi. She agreed the House would pass the Senate bill without any changes if the Senate agreed to pass a separate bill. The second bill was called the *Reconciliation Act of 2010*. The House passed PPACA, the Senate bill, as well as their Reconciliation Act. At that point PPACA was ready for the president to sign, but the Senate still needed to pass the Reconciliation Act from the House.

"The Senate only had fifty-nine votes to pass the Reconciliation Act since Republican Scott Brown replaced Democrat Ted Kennedy. Therefore, in order to pass the Act, Senate Democrats decided to change the rules. They decided to use a different Reconciliation Rule than the House bill, which was only supposed to be used for budget item approvals. Reconciliation wasn't intended to be used for that type of legislation."

"Sounds like a bunch of BS!" I commented.

He said, "It was. Obamacare was unpopular. If Congress hadn't resorted to skullduggery, it would've never passed. Most Americans were against Obamacare."

I asked him, "Why was it so unpopular?"

He said, "People who signed up for Obamacare faced higher premiums, fewer doctors, and skimpier coverages. Premiums for the most popular plans kept rising. Insurers boosted out-of-pocket costs, such as deductibles, copays, and coinsurance.

"Because enrollment was about half of what it was expected to be, the level of enrollment wasn't sustainable. They needed almost twice the number of enrollees to have a viable pool of policyholders with enough healthy people to pay for the sick. The insurance risk pools on the Obamacare exchanges needed a substantial number of young and healthy people to keep premiums from skyrocketing. Only about a quarter of the exchange enrollees were between the ages 18 to 34, far below the 38 to 40 percent needed. The participation of healthy people was vital to offset the cost of sicker people.

"Regulations governing Obamacare exchanges reduced the quality of insurance plans. To cover the cost of the regulations and keep premiums even remotely reasonable, insurers had to increase people's out-of-pocket costs and reduce provider networks. Obamacare eroded choice in the private market and in the healthcare space. Insurance plans sold on government run Obamacare exchanges had fewer hospitals and doctors. Many insurers opted to limit their selection of doctors in some exchange plans to keep premiums and other costs down. Some exchange plans at both the federal and state marketplaces didn't offer access to specialists. New plans offered a narrow network of doctors and facilities. Many policyholders lost their insurance in the individual marketplace because their plans didn't meet Obamacare requirements.

"The *Affordable Care Act* did nothing to curb the price of health insurance. Instead, it subsidized overuse of healthcare under the benefit-rich policies required by the law. The purpose of the new law wasn't to ensure all Americans better healthcare. If it was, pro-Obama business owners, unions, and congressional staffers would have wanted in. Rather, it was a healthcare bureaucracy with more dependents, more federal workers, and higher redistributive taxes."

I asked, "Was there a goal?"

"Yeah," Paul answered. "Increasing the size of government, getting more people on the dole. Options are taken before oppression is given.[221] Cords of restriction are the swords of manipulation.[222] New laws destroy old liberties.[223] Obamacare wasn't about healthcare. It was really about centralized government control. When the federal government took over healthcare it took control of one-sixth of the US economy. One-sixth of America's economy was devoted to medicine. It was all a ruse. Obamacare was designed to fail so we would have a single-payer healthcare system."

I said to him, "Wait a minute! If Obamacare was so bad, why didn't anyone try to stop it?"

"They did," he answered.

"Who?" I asked.

"The *Tea Party*," he replied.

I asked, "What's a tea party?"

He said, "The *Tea Party*. It was a conservative political movement that began on February 19, 2009. An editor for the CNBC Business News Network named Rick Santelli is credited with giving rise to the *Tea Party* movement because he made a reference to the *Boston Tea Party* in response to President Obama's mortgage bailout plan. He declared that America needed 'a new kind of tea party.'

"Tea Partiers opposed excessive taxation and government intervention in the private sector. They were angry and frustrated over the growth of government spending, taxation, and regulation. The *Tea Party* revolution was all about stopping Obamacare." I asked Paul who they were.

He told me, "Most of them were conservative Republicans. Democrats, Libertarians, and Independents were also part of the *Tea Party*. All of them identified with the premises set forth by the US Constitution. The movement found a large and loyal following early on. The *Tea Party* quickly gained traction and supporters. The movement's initial success didn't carry over, however. Many Republicans thought the *Tea Party* was too radical and was costing the GOP votes and seats in Congress. The steepest decline among its supporters was among those who described themselves as moderate or liberal. Five years after it burst onto the national political scene as a grassroots force, the *Tea Party* faded as a national movement."

"So, that was it," I commented.

"No," Paul said. "The party wasn't over. Obamacare faced other challenges."

I asked, "By whom?"

He said, "By plaintiffs. In 2011 the constitutionality of the *Affordable Care Act* was adjudicated. The case was called *National Federal of Independent Business v. Sebelius*.[224] The NFIB argued the individual mandate portion of the *Affordable Care Act* requiring individuals to purchase at least minimal health insurance coverage wasn't a tax and therefore it violated the Constitution. The Obama administration won the case. The Court ruled five to four in favor of Sebelius. Chief Justice John Roberts along with Justices Ruth Bader Ginsburg, Stephen Breyer, Sonia Sotomayor, and Elena Kagan agreed Congress didn't intend that the payment for non-compliance with the Individual Mandate be a tax for purposes of the *Anti-Injunction Act*. They concluded the Individual Mandate penalty is a tax for the purposes of the Constitution's Taxing and Spending Clause[225] and is a valid exercise of congressional authority.

"Justice Roberts wrote:"

> Amicus contends that the Internal Revenue Code treats the penalty as a tax, and that the Anti-Injunction Act therefore bars this suit,[226]

"The challenges to Obamacare weren't over however. The *Affordable Care Act* was tested again in 2015. This time it was *King v. Burwell*.[227] The petitioners argued the law provided eligibility for tax credits only to those persons in states with state-operated exchanges and that the IRS regulation exceeded the agency's statutory authority. The law they claimed violated the *Administrative Procedure Act*.[228] Chief Justice Roberts delivered the opinion for the majority again. The Court in a six to three decision held Congress didn't delegate the authority to determine whether the tax credits are available through both state-created and federally-created exchanges to the Internal Revenue Service. The six justices determined the language of the statute clearly indicated that Congress intended the tax credits to be available through both types of exchanges.

"In both cases the Supreme Court sided with the Obama administration."

I said, "We don't have Obamacare anymore. Do you know why it's gone?"

"I do," Paul answered. "It was its cost. It wasn't a popular uprising or a court case. It was too expensive. It collapsed. The thing was such a mess, it had to be scrapped."

CHAPTER 9

The Pharaoh Who Did Not Know Joseph

Generations that lose their children are followed
by generations that lose their liberty.

I TOLD HIM I'M surprised I never heard any of this before. Then I reminded him he had some unfinished business. I said, "When we first met, you told me, 'Slavery started a chain of events that caused America to go full circle' and that 'slavery for one group of people produced slavery for all people.' Did you forget slavery?"

He answered, "Let's take a break."

I started thinking. *It's obvious the socialists are hiding something.* They're selective. Everything they say is one-sided. There's an agenda here. *Maybe Paul has the answer* I pondered.

A few minutes later he shouted, "I got it! Remember this?" In his hand was the copy of the original *United States Constitution* he had. He had been looking for it while we were taking a breather. After he found it, he placed it in my hands. "Read here," he said.

> The Congress shall have Power To . . . make all Laws which shall be necessary and proper for carrying into Execution the foregoing Powers, and all other Powers vested by this Constitution in the Government of the United States, or in any Department or Officer thereof.[229]

"You want to know when America became a tyranny . . . okay, here it is. It all began when the legislative branch became feckless. I can't give you the exact date when that happened. I can say this, however: the legislative branch was the most important branch of government. All legislative powers granted in the Constitution were vested in the Congress of the United States. I mentioned that earlier. Remember? When the legislative branch became weak, the executive and judicial branches became stronger. The founders intended for there to be three separate but equal branches. Let's recap.

"The legislative branch was made up of the House of Representatives and the Senate. Its main responsibility was to create laws. The executive branch was headed by the president of the United States. Its main responsibility was to enforce the laws the legislative branch created. The judicial branch was the branch of the courts. Its main responsibility was to interpret the laws the legislative branch created. Each branch had its own responsibilities and powers granted by the Constitution. Checks and balances prevented one branch from gaining too much power over the others."

I asked, "Why was the legislative branch so important?"

He said, "The legislative branch was the only branch of government that could make new laws or change existing laws. That didn't stop President Obama, however. He overstepped Congress."

I asked, "How?"

He said, "Whenever President Obama couldn't strike a deal with Congress he wrote an executive order."

I asked, "What's that?"

He said, "They were legally binding orders given by the president and they were steeped in controversy. Every Commander in Chief from George Washington to Mark Duke Bell used them in one form or another. Tens of thousands were issued since 1789. While there was no specific provision that permitted them, there was a 'grant of executive power' given in Article II of the Constitution. Executive branch agencies issued regulations with the full force of law, but these were only under the authority of laws already enacted by Congress. Most of the time they dealt with more mundane matters of bureaucracy, like renaming a park. Sometimes they were used in times of war or to respond to natural disasters or an economic crisis.

"They were controversial because they allowed the president to make major decisions, even law, without the consent of Congress. They didn't require congressional approval, but they had the same legal weight as a law passed by Congress."

"So they were like a decree," I commented.

"Not really," Paul answered. "If Congress didn't like what the president was doing, it had two options. It could rewrite or amend a previous law, or spell it out in greater detail. Congress couldn't directly vote to override an executive order in the way it could a veto. Instead, Congress had to pass a bill canceling or changing the order in a manner it saw fit. The problem with that option was that the president had the right to veto the bill if he disagreed with it. Hence a two-thirds majority was needed to override an executive order. That option wasn't very easy. Congressional cancellations of executive orders were extremely rare.

"The other option was to challenge it in court on the grounds that it deviated from 'congressional intent' or that it exceeded the president's constitutional powers. A lawsuit could be brought if it was felt an order contradicted the legislative intent of the original policy set by Congress or if it had no underlying statutory authority. The Supreme Court could then declare the order unconstitutional."

I asked, "How many executive orders did Obama sign?"

He said, "Compared to Franklin Roosevelt, not many. FDR had the most. I don't know the exact number—I'm pretty sure it was around 300. The number he signed wasn't an issue. The amount of times he exercised executive actions wasn't unprecedented. The problem was that so many were in direct violation or in opposition to the intent of the Congress. Barack Obama abused the executive order process.

"One executive order known as the *Deferred Action for Childhood Arrivals* program was particularly controversial. The action was taken on June 15, 2012 during his second presidential campaign. It allowed people under thirty who came to the United States before the age of sixteen to get a two-year deferral from deportation, under certain conditions."

I said, "Yeah, so?"

"Congress was responsible for crafting the laws that determine how and when noncitizens can become naturalized citizens of the United States! Look!" he shouted.

> The Congress shall have Power To . . . establish an uniform Rule of Naturalization, . . .[230]

"Not only that, the Obama administration decided the *Defense of Marriage Act* was unconstitutional. That decision should've been left to the Supreme Court. See."

> The judicial Power of the United States, shall be vested in one supreme Court, and in such inferior Courts as the Congress may from time to time ordain and establish.[231]

"Obama proved the executive branch could do whatever it wanted and get away with it. We live in an age now where any despot can arbitrarily nullify a law; ignore it; or simply create a new one."

• • •

"Let me get this straight," I argued. "The United States is a tyranny because of the executive branch?"

Paul got up. "No, but you're getting close. One of the three branches is responsible. It wasn't the executive branch, however. Executive orders were reversible. If one president didn't like an order from a previous administration, he could legally cancel it on his own. Besides, Congress could override a presidential veto with a two-thirds majority vote."

I asked, "Was it the legislative branch?"

He said, "It wasn't the legislative branch either. The president had veto power over any law passed by Congress, and the Supreme Court had the power of judicial review. If Congress passed a law that was blatantly unconstitutional, the Supreme Court could overturn it, even if the president had signed it into law."

I told him, "The only branch left is the judicial branch."

"Bingo!" he sounded. "US Supreme Court decisions were constitutionally established to be the supreme law of the land. Look."

> The judicial Power shall extend to all Cases, in Law and Equity, arising under this Constitution, the Laws of the United States, and Treaties made, or which shall be made, under their authority;[232]

He asked, "You ever heard of an oligarchy? It's a government in which a small group exercises control. That's what the Supreme Court was. The nine justices weren't elected officials, yet Supreme Court rulings were the final word on everything. Overturning a Supreme Court decision was very difficult. Supreme Court rulings could only be overturned by the Supreme Court. Not even Congress or the president could override a Supreme Court decision. It was an oligarchy in every sense of the word."

I said, "Tell me more about these justices."

He said, "Okay. They were nominated by the president and confirmed by the Senate. They remained on the bench for the rest of their lives or until they retired. They could stay on the court so long as they displayed good behavior. For all intents and purposes they were appointed for life. The basic purpose of their lifetime appointment was to protect them against unwarranted interference from the legislative and executive branches and so they could make a decision without worrying about being thrown out."

I interrupted. "The United States is a tyranny because of them? How?"

"Because of judicial activism. The people behind the bench became a benchmark."

"What does that mean?" I asked.

He told me, "They had a tendency to legislate from the bench. Judicial activism occurs when judges write subjective policy preferences into the law rather than apply the law impartially according to its original meaning. Take for example *Dred Scott v. Sandford*,[233] better known as the Dred Scott case. Dred Scott, a slave who had lived in the state of Illinois and the territory of Wisconsin with his owner John Emerson before returning to the slave state of Missouri brought the case before the Old Courthouse in St. Louis, Missouri in 1847, thirteen years prior to the Civil War. He argued his time spent in these locations entitled him to emancipation.

"The case was eventually brought before the Supreme Court. Chief Justice Roger B. Taney and six other justices didn't buy Scott's line of reasoning. On March 6, 1857 the Court ruled Scott's time spent in Illinois and the Northwest Territory didn't make him free once he returned to Missouri and as a black man he was excluded from United States citizenship and couldn't therefore bring suit.

"According to them, blacks hadn't been part of the people who made the Constitution. It didn't matter whether they were slaves or freemen, they couldn't expect any protection from the federal government or the courts.

"The Court was on shaky ground, constitutionally speaking," he said. "Its logic on citizenship was convoluted. It did admit blacks could be citizens of a particular state and that they could vote in some states. Nevertheless, it argued state citizenship had nothing to do with national citizenship. Problem was, the Constitution required all states, and by inference the federal government, to afford all persons the same rights. See."

The Citizens of each State shall be entitled to all Privileges and Immunities of Citizens in the several States.[234]

"That included the right to sue in federal court. What's more, Article III didn't mention national citizenship. It established the jurisdiction of the federal courts. The framers wrote:"

> The judicial Power shall extend to all Cases, in Law and Equity, arising under this Constitution, the Laws of the United States, and Treaties made, or which shall be made, under their Authority; . . . to Controversies . . . between two or more States;–[between a State and Citizens of another State;–] between Citizens of different States, . . .[235]

"Slaves were included. They were to be counted in the census with everyone else every ten years, albeit as individuals they were considered three-fifths of the number of 'free persons' of any state."

I asked why that was. "For the purposes of representation," Paul replied.

I said, "Please explain."

He said, "Southerners insisted that slaves be counted with freemen so they'd have more representation in Congress. Founding Fathers James Wilson and Roger Sherman proposed they be counted as three-fifths in total when apportioning representatives, presidential electors, and taxes. The delegates at the *Constitutional Convention* in Philadelphia in 1787 accepted the *Three-Fifths Compromise*. Its implementation gave the Southern States a third more seats in Congress and a third more electoral votes. The agreement greatly increased their representation and political power. If they hadn't reached a settlement, the Constitution wouldn't have been ratified and there wouldn't have been a Union. There wouldn't have been a United States without the Southern States on board.

"The 'three-fifths' clause[236] had nothing to do with race. It wasn't a statement about personhood either. Black slaves weren't being described as 'three-fifths' of a white person. Northern delegates wanted to dilute Southern voting strength. They wanted to outlaw slavery by constitutional means. Slave states in 1793 would've had 33 of the 105 representatives in the House had congressional seats been assigned based on free populations. They had 47 with the compromise. They would've had even more seats and more representation in the Electoral College had slaves been counted the same as freemen. Abolitionist Frederick Douglass, who was black, understood the compromise. He claimed it was 'a downright disability laid upon the slaveholding states.'[237]

"Back to the Dred Scott decision," Paul said. "Chief Justice Taney was a former slave owner from a slave-holding family, as were four other Southern justices on the Court. Those justices and two others had been appointed by pro-slavery presidents from the South. Because of them, slaves were denied their freedom, and black people couldn't exercise their right to claim citizenship. The Court also struck down the *Missouri Compromise* as unconstitutional—a statute passed by Congress that prohibited slavery in the western territories north of the parallel 36°30 north. It ruled the federal government couldn't deprive property owners their right to take their property anywhere in the United States without due process. Not only that, laws that would've freed slaves were barred because of the decision, all but guaranteeing there'd be no political solution to the slavery problem. Dred Scott was a classic case of judicial activism."

• • •

He told me, "That wasn't the only bad decision the Court made. There were others. Take *Buck v. Bell*[238] for example. On May 2, 1927, by a vote of eight to one, the United States Supreme Court upheld a Virginia law that authorized the forced sterilization of 'feeble-minded' persons at certain state institutions. The Buck case was the first time in the Court's history that an intrusive medical procedure was endorsed by the government. Many saw the decision as a validation of negative eugenics.

"The Court ruled the state statute permitting state-enforced sterilization of the genetically unfit 'for the protection and health of the state' didn't violate the Due Process clause of the Fourteenth Amendment to the *United States Constitution*. Writing for the majority, Oliver Wendell Holmes, Jr. described Carrie Buck as the 'probable potential parent of socially inadequate offspring, likewise afflicted.' According to him 'three generations of imbeciles' were enough.

"Upholding Virginia's sterilization statute provided the green light for similar laws in thirty other states. Because of *Buck v. Bell* an estimated 65,000 Americans were sterilized without their own consent or that of a family member. Do you want to hear something ridiculous?" Paul asked.

"What?" I replied.

He said, "In a complete reversal, the Supreme Court invalidated a Texas state law that made it a crime to obtain or attempt an abortion except on medical advice to save the life of the mother. The class action suit was filed by Jane Roe—a pregnant single woman who wanted safely and legally to end her pregnancy."

"Jane Roe," I blurted, "as in *Roe v. Wade*?"

"You're paying attention. That's good," he answered. "The Court struck down the Texas law by a seven to two vote. Remember? The court recognized for the first time that the constitutional right to privacy extended to a woman's right to make her own personal medical decisions—including the decision to have an abortion. The majority of the justices maintained a woman's right to an abortion fell within the right to privacy recognized in *Griswold v. Connecticut*.[239] The Court's ruling was based on the Due Process Clause of the Fourteenth Amendment. Notice in 1973, the Supreme Court recognized a woman's right to an abortion as a fundamental right included within the guarantee of personal privacy."

I replied, "Yeah. So what?"

Paul asked, "Where was Carrie Buck's fundamental right to privacy? In her case the Court sided with the Commonwealth of Virginia. The Virginia statute she sought protection from according eight justices was within the power of the state under the Fourteenth Amendment. The constitutionality of Virginia's law allowing state-enforced sterilization was affirmed."

I said, "What's your point?"

"My point is the Court was inconsistent and political. Explain this?" he asked. "The Supreme Court gave Jane Roe total autonomy over her pregnancy during the first trimester. The decision to have an abortion was left to her and her doctor. The Supreme Court, on the other hand, ordered that Carrie Buck be sterilized under the *Virginia Eugenical Sterilization Act*.[240] She was the first person in Virginia sterilized under the new law."

"That's one example. Let's look at another: the first case *Korematsu v. United States*.[241] The Petitioner was a United States citizen of Japanese descent named Fred Korematsu. He was ordered out of his home and was sent to an internment camp in the Utah desert."

I stopped him. "You said, 'Times were different back then.' That kind of thing happened before the Revolution?"

"It did," Paul remarked. "Two months after the Japanese bombing of Pearl Harbor, on December 7, 1941, President Franklin Roosevelt issued Executive Order 9066, which permitted the military to circumvent the constitutional safeguards of ordinary American citizens in the name of national defense. In the next six months Japanese-Americans were moved from the West Coast to assembly hubs farther inland. They were then evacuated to isolated sites, known as War Relocation Centers. By June, approximately 122,000 Japanese-Americans, including children, were relocated to these remote camps built by the US military in scattered locations around the country.

"Korematsu refused to leave his home in San Leandro, California. In 1942 he was arrested and was charged with violating the military's exclusion order. Later on he was convicted in a federal district court. Duly convicted, he appealed. In 1944 his case reached the Supreme Court."

"Let me guess," I interjected. "The Court sided with the government."

"You're a quick study," he replied. "His conviction was upheld on the grounds of military necessity. The Supreme Court, in a six to three vote, held that the wartime internment of American citizens of Japanese descent during World War II was constitutional, that the need to protect against espionage outweighed the individual rights of American citizens. Justice Hugo Black delivered the opinion of the Court. He argued that compulsory exclusion, though constitutionally suspect, was justified during circumstances of 'emergency and peril.'

"Here's the thing," Paul declared. "Foreign prisoners had rights under the Constitution. Let's look at another case. The case was *Boumediene v. Bush*.[242] Lakhdar Boumediene and six other Algerians who were being held by the United States as terror suspects filed a *habeas corpus* petition in a US federal court. They were arrested in Bosnia and Herzegovina on suspicion of plotting to attack the US embassy in Sarajevo. Later, they were handed over to the US and imprisoned at the Guantanamo Bay detention camp in Cuba.

"A US District Court in Washington D.C. ruled that the detainees didn't have *habeas corpus* rights. The Supreme Court in 2008 reversed the lower court decision. It ruled that the nearly six hundred men imprisoned at Guantanamo had a constitutional right to go to federal court to challenge their detention. The legal provisions that had suspended this right were found to be unconstitutional. Writing for the five–four majority Justice Kennedy said, 'The laws and Constitution are designed to survive, and remain in force, in extraordinary times.'"

• • •

I didn't want to hear about court cases anymore, so I stopped him before he said anything else. "There must've been a tipping point. Exactly when did America become a tyranny? How many times do I have to ask?"

"You want to know when America changed. Is that it?" Paul answered. I told him, "Yes!"

"When the rule of law was replaced by the rule of men. Civilizations unravel as soon as they unravel the rule of law.[243] Economic and political situations improve, though once the rule of law has been tampered with, corruption is practically unavoidable.[244]

"Stable civilizations are built upon a strong covenant between the people and their government. The role of government is to protect the people from injustice, and the role of the people is to obey the law. Whenever either side breaks its agreement, the system no longer works.[245] Wherever law is unpredictable, peace is unobtainable.[246] Wrested judgment creates unrest.[247] Order follows the following of statutory law."[248]

I said, "Here we go again . . . more adages."

"Here's my point," he declared. "America was a judicial tyranny. Then it became a socialist dictatorship."

I told him, "I'm listening."

"Overriding the Constitution was easy," he said. "All you had to do was appoint an activist judge."

"It was that simple?" I remarked.

"Yeah," he answered. "When opinions become the law of the land, the land becomes subject to vanity, and when evil men judge, evil becomes law.[249] America had an Achilles Heel. It was the Supreme Court."

I said, "What do you mean?"

"The Justices," he announced.

"What about them?"

"They were affected by public opinion. Supreme Court justices made decisions based on their personal politics. Problem was you couldn't stop them. Impeaching justices was virtually impossible unless they broke the law. Congress had the authority to remove them from office by impeachment proceedings, but that didn't happen very often. The only Justice who was impeached was Associate Justice Samuel Chase in 1805. The House of Representatives passed Articles of Impeachment against him. He was acquitted by the Senate.

"There was one other option. An amendment could be proposed by two-thirds of both houses of Congress, or by two-thirds of the state legislatures. Remember? Amending the Constitution was difficult. It required a supermajority of either members of Congress or of state legislatures. Once the bill passed both houses, the proposed amendment had to go to the individual states for their consideration. It then had to be ratified by seventy-five percent of the states, either by their legislatures or state constitutional conventions. Thirty-three amendments received a two-thirds vote from both the House of Representatives and the Senate. Only twenty-seven of those were ratified by the States.

"The Supreme Court was just another federal legislature. The only difference was its justices weren't elected officials. Now back to your question," he cried out. "'When did America became a tyranny,' you ask. It was at the end of the 20th century. You ever heard of political correctness?"

I said, "No. What's that?"

Paul pulled out a dictionary. He said, "Here's its definition:"

> agreeing with the idea that people should be careful to not use language or behave in a way that could offend a particular group of people[250]

"The term 'political correctness' dates back a long way," he said. "It was used infrequently until the latter part of the 20th century. The expression had more mainstream usage in America in the 1980's and 90's. From college campuses it began spreading throughout the whole society—sort of like relativism.

"Do you want to know what it really means?" he asked.

I said, "Please, tell me."

"It's Marxism translated from economic into cultural terms. It's the primary vehicle by which viewpoints not in line with an established way of thinking are eliminated."

"Political correctness?" I commented. "America is a tyranny because of that?"

"Yes," he answered.

I said, "How?"

"Americans are afraid to speak out because of it. They're fearful of using the wrong word. They don't want to be called racist, xenophobic, sexist, or homophobic. You have to be careful nowadays. If you say the 'wrong thing,' you could be penalized, fired, or even taken to prison."

• • •

I said, "Now we're getting somewhere. Political correctness is designed to eliminate competition."

"Yes," he replied. "It seeks to repress free speech."

I told him, "I get it now. I've seen it myself. It's an established ortho-doxy. We need to fight back!"

"That's harder than you think," he said. "If you're politically incorrect, you fall into the social pariah category because you're not using the appro-priate PC terminology. Anyone who doesn't conform is labeled a heretic. If the truth isn't politically correct, you can be ostracized for speaking it. There isn't a political solution anymore."

I asked, "How did this happen?"

He said, "It didn't happen all at once. It happened steadily over time. The first victims were Christians."

I said, "How were they victims?" He didn't respond right away.

Seconds later he told me, "It was their objection to same-sex marriage. Secular humanists wanted it, and Christians stood in the way. The perse-cution of Christians in the United States, particularly those who opposed same-sex marriage, began in 2015. You'll never guess who was responsible."

"Who was it?" I queried.

He paused. "It was the Supreme Court. The case was *Obergefell v. Hodges*.[251] Five justices who were on the Court in 2015 bypassed the legisla-tive process altogether. They took it upon themselves to impose same-sex marriage on America—something which was rejected for thousands of years by every nation on earth until then.

"The ruling did a lot to undermine religious liberty. Redefining mar-riage led straight to the persecution of Christians. The ruling in favor of gay marriage led to widespread animosity and legal battles. Christian owned bakeries were getting death threats for refusing to make wedding cakes for same-sex couples. Some of them were forced to go out of business. Teachers were suspended for expressing anti-gay marriage views on their own time, and religious universities were forced to allow same-sex couples in their married dormitories.

"Christians weren't the only ones affected. Orthodox Jews and Mus-lims, even atheists were embattled. They became bigots as well. Believe me there was nothing worse back then than being called a bigot."

I replied, "No one helped?"

He said, "They tried. State legislatures passed religious freedom laws. It didn't matter though because the courts overturned them."

• • •

"From there things got worse," he said.

I asked, "In what way?"

"The Millennial Generation," he replied.

I said, "What's that?"

"It's a group of people," Paul answered.

I said, "What about them?"

He said, "They're folks born between 1980 and 2000. It's the generation that followed Generation X. They were the first generation to come of age in the new millennium. People thought they were slackers because they had a reputation as being self-absorbed. They were often described as spoiled with a poor work ethic and disconnected. They were called 'the entitled generation.' Truth be told, they've gotten a bad rap. Millennials grew up in a world that was very different from any group before them."

I asked, "How so?"

He said, "Millennials had less opportunity than any previous generation. They earned less than their parents, had fewer job prospects, and they were less likely to be homeowners. I already told you finding an affordable place to live was hard, especially if you were just starting out.

"More of them were living in poverty and fewer were employed. Many Millennials grew up during the *Great Recession*. Education was very expensive. A good portion of them were under heavy college debt. They couldn't afford healthcare either. It was tougher for Millennials to get started than it was for prior generations."

He looked over at me. "I want to be clear. They weren't helpless by any means. They had less help. They relied on their families for financial aid because they couldn't find a job. Besides, the *Great Recession* undercut their faith in the free market system. They knew their futures were likely to be far less bright than their parents' and grandparents'. Is it any wonder the Millennial Generation was infatuated with socialism?"

I said, "They liked socialism?"

"Of course they did," he responded. "They had absolutely no idea what it was. They didn't live through the *Cold War*. They hadn't heard much about the Soviet Union. Nobody told them about Soviet atrocities. Joseph Stalin was worse than Adolf Hitler! He ordered the execution of thirty thousand Russian officers because he was worried some of them might challenge his stranglehold on power and millions died as a result of his farm policy. The man was worse than Hitler because his regime killed far more people, tens of millions. Historians estimate twenty million Soviet citizens were eradicated. The majority of those deaths were caused by neglect or repressive policies.

"There's more. The Soviet Union had adopted a formal position of state-atheism after the Bolshevik Revolution. Why? Because Christianity was a threat. There was no greater threat to religious liberty in the 20th century than atheistic communism."

I said, "Nobody told me."

"The Soviet Union fell apart fifty-seven years ago. I bet they didn't tell you that either," Paul reacted. "Marxism-Leninism was dumped unceremoniously. You see, Tim, Marxist Socialism is government control of the economy! It doesn't work! The Soviet system had many problems. The main problem was lack of productivity. Communism failed to provide incentives for workers and citizens to work. The country couldn't feed itself. People had to wait in long lines just to buy bread. Millennials weren't aware! Schools were force-feeding them left-wing propaganda instead of facts. Unfortunately, American schools taught very little about basic economic theory."

• • •

"Millennials grew up. In 2032 they were the majority."

I replied, "That's the year all hell broke loose."

He said, "You're right. 2032 was a pivotal year. America's financial chickens came home to roost. The United States couldn't meet its debt obligation. It couldn't get a low-interest rate from lenders because investors were concerned the US couldn't afford to pay the bonds. The value of bonds started decreasing. Fears about the economy caused investors to dump treasuries. Markets around the world started plunging. This prompted interest rates around the world to spike. The dollar dropped, as investors fled and the greenback lost its status as a global world currency.

"Investors tried to get their hands on money wherever they could find it. Financial markets started sinking and bank lending to the private sector stopped. The unemployment rate kept climbing and the drop in stock prices hurt many Americans' retirement accounts. The economy slipped into the biggest depression ever. The market didn't recover. America was in terrible shape. Social Security checks were delayed. The US government couldn't pay salaries or benefits for federal or military personnel. Non-essential services were shut down altogether."

I asked, "Why did everything collapse?"

He said, "Because the politicians dug themselves a hole. They promised us many things they couldn't deliver—like free education, free healthcare, free housing, and so many other things. Nothing is free. Those things cost money!"

"Those things are free," I told him. "I never paid for any of them."

With frustration in his voice he said, "Somebody is paying for them. If it isn't you, it's someone else. Before wealth can be redistributed, it has to be created. One man's security is another man's liability."[252]

"That's true," I replied.

"You know what else is true?" Paul asked.

I said, "No. Tell me."

"Governing is difficult. It's even harder when the people you're governing are bi-polar. Safety nets are essential! Funding them is another matter entirely! No one wants to pay for them, particularly if they're for someone else!

"The people must own up to government ownership.[253] The federal government couldn't keep its financial house in order. It tried many times. It couldn't however, because voters kept getting in the way. You see, Tim, voters rain down opposition every time politicians rein in spending.[254] If their constituents do not curb their appetite for government programs, elected officials cannot curb the size of government.[255]

"Here's a famous quote attributed to Alexander Fraser Tytler, a British lawyer and writer from Scotland." Paul paused for a moment to retrieve the document from his secret chamber, and then he pulled it out and put it in my hand.

> A democracy cannot exist as a permanent form of government. It can only exist until the people discover they can vote themselves largess out of the public treasury. From that moment on, the majority always votes for the candidate promising the most benefits from the public treasury, with the result that democracy always collapses over a loose fiscal policy—to be followed by a dictatorship.[256]

I said, "You have a knack Paul . . . you never fail to amaze me. One question though; the politicians, you know Democrats and Republicans, if they knew what was going to happen, why did they keep kicking the can down the road?"

"Excellent question," he remarked. "They were stuck between a rock and a hard place. They couldn't cut spending because there were too many folks on the dole. They had to increase spending every year, or risk a back-lash. Once a government program is started, it's tough to repeal it."

"That makes sense," I replied. "Be that as it may, I believe they could've done something to balance the budget."

He said, "Not really . . . not if they wanted to win reelection. Their only interest was getting votes. Fixing problems wasn't high up on the list. They were constantly vying for reelection."

• • •

"After the collapse officials at the Treasury Department found them-selves in a position where they couldn't repay the principal and interest on the national debt. They decided they were better off not paying it at all. The United States went into default."

"Default?" I replied.

"Yeah; the country couldn't pay its creditors on time. It's the national equivalent of going bankrupt."

I said, "It went bankrupt? Why?"

"Because taxes weren't bringing in enough revenue. The US Treasury couldn't cover its monthly payments. Do you know why that happened?"

I told him, "No, but I bet you're gonna tell me."

"You're right," he responded. "It happened because the federal gov-ernment was spending more money than it was taking in. Families were more dependent on government programs than ever before. Nearly three-quarters of all US households—about seventy-one percent were dependent on the state. Entitlement spending was soaking up all federal revenue.

"Remember when I said, 'There's less money in the economy for consumers and for businesses when bureaucrats waste it, and there's less economic activity and fewer jobs.'"

I said, "Yeah."

"Washington's overspending was severely impacting economic growth. The bottom had fallen out of the American economy . . . worst of all, 2032 was an election year."

I said, "What do you mean?"

He told me, "Forty-nine days after the US defaulted, Mark Duke Bell entered the presidential race."

"Our shepherd?" I reacted.

"Yes," he said. "On February 27, 2032 he announced he was running for president."

"He wasn't always in charge?" I replied.

"No. He wasn't always in control," Paul clarified. "Before he was America's dictator, Mark Duke Bell worked in Silicon Valley. He made billions off of his hi-tech ventures. Folks called him the Antioch Epiphany because he was born in Antioch, California, and because he was so striking. The guy was a huge celebrity. You ever heard of Duralonics?"

I said, "No. What's that?"

"It's a company. Bell is one of its co-founders. Let me show you." Paul reached into his secret chamber again. He looked especially determined this time, as if he had something really important to show me.

"Bell rose from obscurity to become the most powerful man in America. Though he was a minor player in the tech-world early in his career, Bell became a prominent executive in 2025. In July that year he was elevated to president and CEO of Pantheon Global."

I asked, "Is that significant?"

He said, "Of course. Pantheon Global is a huge international banking firm located in San Francisco with affiliates all over the globe. Its partners manage the financial needs of their own clients, and together they're amalgamated into one giant conglomerate. Pantheon Global's motto is 'Dedicated to the Veneration of Every Imagination.'"

I told him, "It says here he created the WICAN platform."

He said, "That's correct. Bell left Pantheon Global in 2027. He joined Duralonics shortly thereafter and became a co-founder, along with Ashur Malik, Carlos Angel, and Anton Eckhart. They're the architects of WICAN."

I said, "According to this article it's some sort of banking system."

"It's not any banking system," he responded. "It's worldwide."

I asked him, "How does it work?"

His reply came without hesitation. "WICAN stands for 'World International Commerce Access Network.' It's a cooperative society owned by Duralonics. Duralonics assigns each member a unique number that corresponds with his or her name. Every member pays a one-time fee at the beginning, plus annual charges. Duralonics also charges users for financial transactions.

"It's a universal network that allows banks and other institutions around the world to send and receive money in a fast and stable environment. It oversees the vast and complicated web of unique identifier codes I just mentioned. Without it we wouldn't have one global economy."

• • •

Paul turned his head toward the door as if he were trying to hear something. He kept eyeing the entrance. I looked at him. "Paul—is everything okay?" He said everything's fine. I could see something was bothering him, but I couldn't hear what it was. After a brief pause he resumed like nothing happened.

"He's crafty."

"Who's that?" I replied.

"Mark Duke Bell. Who do you think? Anastatia Matsin never knew what hit her."

"Never heard of her," I responded.

He said, "She was president of the United States when the bottom fell out of the US economy. She couldn't have been president at a worse time. She has an incredible story though.

"Anastatia Matsin was born on November 9, 1979, in Germantown, Illinois. She graduated top of her class at Yale University and went on to Harvard Business School. After earning an MBA she moved to San Francisco, and joined Pantheon Global, where she later became chairwoman."

I commented, "The same Pantheon Global where Bell worked?"

"Yes," he said. "She was on the board of directors. She was an executive in the banking industry and was on several boards. Before she was president of the Unite States, she was a businesswoman turned politician.

"She served as governor of Texas from 2025 to 2028. In 2027, she decided to run for president. On March 13, 2027, she announced before a crowd in Houston that she would seek the Democratic Party's presidential nomination. She immediately became the favorite to win. After a contentious series of state primary elections, she won the nomination—a year later she won the presidency."

I said, "Before you continue, may I ask you a question?"

"Of course," Paul replied.

"When you said she 'never knew what hit her' what did you mean by that?"

"I'll show you," he said. He had some papers in his pocket. When I saw them he pulled them out.

"What are those?" I asked.

He said, "They're newspaper clippings from 2032. They explain everything. The economic crisis hit her pretty hard. Foreign countries stopped buying US Treasuries. To make matters worse, the Federal Reserve Bank was out of ammunition. The Chairman of the Federal Reserve said, 'New rounds of quantitative easing will create more inflation. Printing money is absolutely the worst thing we can do.' The Federal Reserve Bank's ability to help the economy was limited. Interest rates were already at or near zero.

"There was fighting amongst progressives over how to deal with the problem. They didn't know what to do next!"

I said, "Let me see that." Paul handed me the newspaper articles. "You're right . . . it says here socialists within her party became unruly."

"Keep reading," he admonished.

"This article says rioting broke out. It also says clashes erupted between police and activists. Thousands of anti-government protesters tried to force their way through police barricades. Whoa!" I shouted. "Federal buildings, and several private businesses were destroyed. Here's a picture of a demonstrator brutally attacking an onlooker in New York. According to this, major riots broke out in thirty-four cities during the course of the year, including in Washington, D.C., New York, Los Angeles, Chicago, Dallas, San Francisco, and Seattle. The violence was widespread."

Paul turned his head toward the door again. He looked unsettled this time, like he was expecting something.

I said, "Why are you looking at the door?"

"No reason," he replied.

I asked, "Are you sure?"

Without missing a beat he said, "It's nothing. Let's focus on the articles.

"State troopers were deployed to large metropolitan areas to help clear protesters. It didn't work however. The number of protests kept growing day by day."

I told him, "I don't see that anywhere." He reached into his pocket again. Inside was another article, which he placed into my hand. I started reading.

I saw the name Edger Nu. The article said he was House Speaker when all this was happening. That he went to President Matsin and proposed she declare martial law. Her response, "Not while I'm president. We've never declared martial law in the past. It was instituted on the national level only once, during the Civil War. We don't have to take such drastic measures right now."

"The next part is crucial," Paul said as he took the article back. "A week later on February 4th a bill was passed in the House. It was called the Protection of People and Property and Stability Act, or PPPSA. The bill placed restrictions on the press and authorized the police to ban political meetings and demonstrations. It was essentially guaranteed to pass, because anything less would have caused the government to implode. Speaker Nu called it, 'One of the most important pieces of legislation to come before Congress in decades.'

"A few days later Senate Majority Leader Earl Ikner said the Senate would take up the bill passed by the House of Representatives before the end of the month. New provisions were added. The Senate bill had even more restrictions than the House bill. It gave the federal government the authority to overrule state and local laws. It voided many key civil liberties. Later on it was used as the legal basis for the imprisonment of anyone considered to be an opponent of the state."

Paul gave me the article again. "Look here," he said. "The president immediately threatened to veto the bill."

"Was it the start of the dictatorship?" I interjected.

"It wasn't," he said. "Read."

According to the article, the bill was very unpopular. President Matsin said "it went too far." Senate Minority Leader Guy King went to her and complained. He told her, "Majority Leader Ikner has no intention of abiding by the law. He intends only to use the new rules legally to establish a dictatorship as quickly as possible."

President Matsin was outraged. Incensed by Ikner's conduct she put together enough votes in the Senate to block passage of the bill. The article said the Senate failed to reach the sixty-vote threshold for cloture. There weren't enough votes to move it forward. Majority Leader Ikner was at a loss. He didn't have the votes needed to override a presidential veto.

• • •

After I finished the article I gave it back to Paul. I told him, "That was the last news story. What happened next?"

"It isn't," he replied. "I have one more document I want to show you. Before I give it to you, please promise me something."

"What?" I retorted.

"Promise me you won't speak about it here in prison."

I told him, "Of course!"

"What you are about to see," he said, "you can't tell anyone about it. It's top secret."

I cried out, "Just give it to me!"

Paul stood. Then he went to his secret chamber again to get the document out. "Nobody knows it's here," he said. "I hid it in a place I knew they'd never look."

I asked him, "What is it?"

"It's an email exchange between Senate Majority Leader Earl Ikner and Mark Duke Bell," he answered.

"How did you get it?" I asked.

He said, "That's not important right now. We need to focus on its content. Senator Ikner went to Bell and asked him if he'd run for president. Bell came back to Ikner with a deal. He accepted on the condition he be named the supreme leader. Ikner went back to Bell. He told him, 'If you defeat President Matsin, you'll be our leader for the rest of your life.' See for yourself."

Ikner

I can't make this deal on my own. I have to get more senators to agree. Some of them oppose the idea. They're afraid Matsin will win.

Bell

Look what's going on! Matsin can't win!

Ikner

I have a plan. I called all the socialists in the Senate together. The riots will continue. We can incite them.

Bell

Take advantage of the crisis. Don't waste this opportunity.

Ikner

Will you sign PPPSA?

Bell

I'll sign it.

Ikner

What about the corporate CEOs?

Bell

They're on board. Don't worry.

Ikner

It's a new era. We can establish a socialist majority. It took generations, but we're finally here. If you defeat President Matsin, you'll be our leader for the rest of your life.

I said, "That's pretty damning."

"If the socialists find out about it, we're in a lot of trouble," Paul alluded. "Bell is their leader. They think he's some kind of a messiah. He said he would 'establish order amongst the ranks.'

"President Matsin sabotaged the Protection of People and Property and Stability Act! She was in the way. They said she was 'a right-wing co-conspirator' and called for her to 'do more to fight poverty and injustice.' All this was happening while America was on fire.

"After Bell became the New Socialist Party nominee, President Matsin was left alone to face him in the general election. The contest that followed wasn't fair."

I stopped him again. "It wasn't fair. Why wasn't it fair?"

"Simple," he answered. "The media was in the tank for Bell. He received far better news coverage than Matsin. Look at the articles I gave you."

I didn't respond. I picked up the newspaper clippings and started to read.

I told him, "You're right. She's a 'rich unsympathetic capitalist diametrically opposed to change' according to this one. This one's pretty bad. Here's a picture of her with a Hitler mustache."

I read some more. The articles were scathing. Nothing Matsin did was acceptable. One journalist wrote, "The meltdown was her fault." Another said, "The rioters are innocent . . . she's to blame." I couldn't make heads or tails of what they were saying. Finally, I asked Paul if any of it was true.

He told me, "It's a bunch of nonsense! The financial meltdown wasn't her fault. It began in 1985 when The United States became the world's largest debtor nation. The riots weren't her fault either. You read the email. She's a scapegoat. The entire world was on Bell's side. Is it any wonder he beat her?"

CHAPTER 10

The Revolution

The difference between sedition and revolution:
the number involved in the evolution.

PAUL TORE UP THE document and flushed it down the toilet. "Did you hear that?" he asked. "Sounds like they're shutting down for the night. Put everything away." I gathered all the papers that were lying around and handed them to him.

He said, "We'll continue in the morning." With those words I sensed it was time to go to sleep.

• • •

I had another dream that night. It was like the one I had dreamed the night before . . . only this time, the man was alive. The tomb they put Him in was empty.

I saw ten men standing before Him. "Peace be unto you," the man said. Then He told them, "All things must be fulfilled, which were written concerning Me. I had to suffer and to rise from the dead the third day." They were all glad.

Then I saw eleven men on a mountain. They were the man's friends. The man was there on that mountain with them. Before He left He said, "Go and teach all nations. I am with you always, even unto the end of the world."

The next day I woke to the sound of the cell door opening. It was the guards. They were doing their regular morning routine. Paul looked scared, but after one of them said, "It's time for breakfast" he got up.

There was something different about him that day. His countenance had changed the night before. He seemed more cautious. The whole time we were eating, he didn't say a word. I asked if everything was okay. He wouldn't reply. Along the way back to our cell I asked him again, "Is everything okay?"

He whispered, "Not now. Be quiet." Normally he would answer me. He didn't that morning for some reason. However, the minute we were back in our cell he began to speak.

• • •

"We can talk now," he said.

I told him, "Continue where you left off."

"With Bell?" he asked.

"Yes, with Bell," I said with frustration.

"The socialists won. They got what they wanted. On February 4, 2033, Bell signed the Protection of People and Property and Stability Act. It was his first act as president . . . it was a new era, indeed. The law was followed by more dramatic and permanent suspensions of civil rights. Eventually all legislative powers were transferred to the executive branch."

I replied, "Yesterday, you told me the executive branch wasn't responsible!"

"That's true. I did say that," he remarked. "I also said, 'When the legislative branch becomes weak, the executive and judicial branches become strong.' Remember?

"The 123rd Congress was a rubber-stamp congress. Bell was given carte blanche to enact his agenda. The Protection of People and Property and Stability Act was just the beginning. More legislation followed. The Harmony and Tolerance Act was signed a week later."

I interrupted. "You mean the Bell Doctrine—no one has the right to make you feel wrong."

"Precisely," Paul responded.

I asked, "What is it exactly?"

He said, "Let me get the articles out again."

• • •

While Paul was searching through his secret chamber I had time to think. I considered the second dream. It was even harder to understand than the first one. None of it made sense. Who were the other men? Where did the man go? How did He rise from the dead? He had to suffer?

Fifteen minutes went by. I said, "What are you looking for?"

He answered, "There're more articles in here. I'm looking for the one about Harmony and Tolerance. Here it is. I knew I had it," he said a few minutes later.

I asked him if I could see it. He walked over with the article in his hand. "Go ahead, read it," he said. Immediately, I noticed the headline.

> The Rights Of Individuals Are Superseded By The Overall Good Of The State.

And then I read more.

> . . . The new law which adds to existing hate crime statutes grants the federal government the authority to regulate hate speech . . . There has not been a moment like this in America since 1791. All men are equal now. They are endowed with certain rights, that among these are life, harmony and the pursuit of tolerance . . .

I said, "That's not such a bad thing. Tolerance is good. Don't you agree?"

"That all depends," he answered.

"On what?" I asked.

He paused. "On your definition. Tolerance means sympathy or indulgence for beliefs or practices differing from or conflicting with one's own.[257] It doesn't mean the same thing anymore. Keep reading."

> . . . Intolerance is intolerable. There is a movement underway to target and eradicate unpopular and offensive ideas in America . . . "Getting rid of harassing hate speech based on race, gender, sexual orientation, immigration status, or any other characteristic is very important," said President Bell. "It's the first step toward true democracy. We must stop people from voicing their opinions, if their opinions harm other people. Tolerance is crucial. Harmony is more important than sovereignty . . ."

"See that. 'Intolerance is intolerable.' That statement violates itself. You cannot force someone to be tolerant without being intolerant toward their intolerance.[258] It's a trick. They're pulling the old bait-and-switch. Read it again. Notice Bell's words."

... Getting rid of harassing hate speech ... is very important ...

"Then he says:"

... Harmony is more important than sovereignty ...

"He baits us in with tolerance, and then switches from tolerance to tyranny. I told you he's crafty."

I sat there dumbfounded.

"You look stunned," Paul remarked.

I told him, "I can't wrap my head around this ... tolerance is tyranny?"

He asked, "Can a tolerant society tolerate intolerance?"

I replied, "That's a good question. I don't think so."

"Right!" he shouted. "Tolerating all together is altogether intolerable![259] Karl Popper summed it up":

> Less well known is the paradox of tolerance: Unlimited tolerance must lead to the disappearance of tolerance. If we extend unlimited tolerance even to those who are intolerant, if we are not prepared to defend a tolerant society against the onslaught of the intolerant, then the tolerant will be destroyed, and tolerance with them.[260]

I gave the paper with the quote on it back and said, "I get it now—tolerance requires differences of opinion. We can't tolerate something unless we disagree with it, and we don't tolerate people we agree with. Tolerance isn't approval or agreement. It's the ability to live with or put up with something."

"That's correct," Paul answered.

I told him, "Socialists are afraid of their own ideology. Modern multiculturalism is monoculturalism."[261]

"Exactly!" he replied. "False liberals question every idea, except their own ideas. They tolerate anything as long as it fits their way of thinking. Look what else Popper said:"

> We should therefore claim, in the name of tolerance, the right not to tolerate the intolerant. We should claim that any movement preaching intolerance places itself outside the law, and we should consider incitement to intolerance and persecution as criminal, in the same way as we should consider incitement to murder, or to kidnapping, or to the revival of the slave trade, as criminal.[262]

"The goal is absolute power. Elitist thugs have it now, and they intend to use it as a weapon ... ask any Christian."

I said, "What do you mean?"

He looked at me. "The Harmony and Tolerance Law has hate speech restrictions on freedom of expression. Public speech against any group where such incitement is likely to lead to a breach of the peace is against the law in the United States. Those convicted of promoting hate are fined and their names are made public. Look at the article. Sermons are subject to the law's restrictions, and pastors are fair targets for criminal prosecution. If you preach the Gospel in a way that violates the law, you will go to jail. You could be put on trial as an enemy of the state."

I waited for him to say something else, but he was silent. "Is there more?" I asked. He didn't respond. I saw him looking at the door again, so I waited.

He said, "If I tell you something, promise me you won't say a word."

I asked, "What is it?"

"Mark Duke Bell is an old acquaintance of mine." I was speechless.

After I regained my composure I said, "For such an influential guy, very little is known about him."

"That's because so-called journalists are doing their best to protect him. Pure objectivity is a rarity.[263] News and shoes are subject to tailoring.[264] Wherever agendas are present, information is missing,"[265] he explained.

I asked him what Bell was like. He said, "He's like a whitewashed tomb: he looks beautiful on the outside, but on the inside he's full of dead men's bones. Bell's public image is that of an angel of light. Behind closed doors he's a different person entirely. Beware of him—he's a wolf in sheep's clothing.

"You see, Tim, he wants the public square entirely to himself. Socialists hate competition. Bell's no exception. Everything he does is done for political reasons. He's Machiavellian."

I asked, "What else do you know?"

"His wife Yasmine is a militant secularist. She hates Christianity. Here's something mainstream media outlets won't tell you. She said, 'I'd like to see it eliminated from public life entirely.'"

I said, "She's Yuri Baleth's daughter. She goes by the name Jessica."

"Yeah, how do you know that?" Paul reacted. I told him I attended the Yuri Baleth Academy in Darby, Pennsylvania.

"You went to one of his schools?" he asked.

"I attended state-run schools set up for troubled youths. I told you that."

He cried out, "You didn't tell me you were a student at a GSB Academy!"

"Does it matter?" I said inquisitively.

"Definitely! They're fronts."

I replied, "What's that?"

He said, "Front groups are organizations that claim to represent one agenda when in reality they serve some other interest whose backing is unseen! Their names suggest academic or political neutrality, while in fact they're funded by powerful industry lobbyists.

"GSB schools get their funding from Baleth, who pretends to be for democracy. He's really acting on behalf of Bell's socialist government. The money is funneled through a worldwide network started by Baleth called the Futurist Society Organization.

"The curriculum at GSB academies, as you probably know, is biased. It's a one-size-fits-all, top-down program that ignores vital history—like the founding of this country, the *Declaration of Independence*, and the Constitution. Attention is lavished on minor historical figures instead.

"The teachers at these educational institutions are espoused to a Marxist political ideology. They use the education system to erode the moral backbone and judgment skills of schoolchildren."

I said, "No wonder I haven't heard any of this."

"The purpose behind state education," he said, "is to detach children from the ethics they learned from their parents so they will be open to a new set of ethical standards. It's a way to turn students against Judeo-Christian principles and Western Civilization. We talked about the public school system the other day. Didn't I say it's, 'Been turning students into useful idiots for a long time?'"

I replied, "You did. You never told me I was one of them."

• • •

Paul said, "What do you know about the food shortages?" I told him there hadn't been enough food for as long as I could remember.

He said, "Yeah, but do you know why?" I didn't say anything.

"You don't want to answer?" he asked. "Bad economics is causing the shortage. America was one of the most prosperous nations in the world. Today, Americans can't even afford basic staples, such as food. When I made $200,000 a year I spent around five percent of my annual salary on groceries. Now someone making $200,000 a year spends his entire paycheck on food."

139

I said, "That's quite a difference." He began to laugh.

"That's because this country doesn't have enough food to feed its population. There aren't enough farms to meet the demand."

I asked, "Why aren't there enough farms?"

He said, "Good question. Take a gander at this headline."

Federal Government Poised To Take Over Food Industry

I looked at him. "The food industry was private?"

"It sure was," he reacted. "It was nationalized in 2033. The United States was running out of food. Prices were skyrocketing, and people were going hungry. Read the article."

> May 13, 2033 "A state of emergency" was issued today . . . The decree gives the federal government extra powers to deal with the ongoing food crisis, including the right to seize private property . . .

"More than eighty thousand farms were confiscated."

I asked, "For what purpose?"

He said, "To create large new agricultural cooperatives. They thought they could increase the food supply for the urban population by replacing commercial farms with collective ones. The goal was to reduce the economic power of private farms. According to Bell, 'Businesses were putting their own interests before the good of the nation.'"

Paul asked for the article. He had another one for me.

I asked him, "How many do you have?"

He said, "Quite a few. I kept as many as I could. This one's pretty important."

> . . . Large metropolitan areas are being supplied with extra food, but there is a great financial crisis in America's farming communities . . . Farmers who have to sell essentials to the state went on strike last Thursday after the government froze food prices . . . The farmers are claiming they cannot make a profit . . .

I told him, "That doesn't sound like success. The farmers went on strike."

He said, "The program was designed to redistribute agricultural produce—in that regard it was a huge success. Quotas were being met initially. Then again, production was disrupted. Government bureaucrats couldn't run farms effectively . . . that caused a decrease in total output. When it was all said and done there was a huge loss in productivity."

I looked at him again, "What happened? Grandma told me there was plenty of food in the past."

"One word . . . socialism," he said without hesitation. "The food that was attained for the cities decreased from 70 billion pounds in 2033 to 64.5 in 2034. Yields fell as incentives to work were removed. Thousands of farmers had to scale back production or stop planting altogether."

I asked, "Why did they do that?"

He paused. "Because they weren't getting paid enough—nobody wanted to farm because there was no money to be made."

I told him, "That doesn't make any sense. The goal of socialism is social equality."

He said, "Not according to Lenin. He said, 'The goal of socialism is communism.'"[266]

I shouted, "You mean it doesn't work!"

"True socialism never works," he alleged. "It only works when it's not worked into the economy. The purpose of socialism is socialism. It's a political movement."

I asked him, "Then who does it benefit?"

He got up from his bunk. "Government benefits from socialism, not the consumer.[267] Take the healthcare system, for example. It's like a parent-child relationship . . . every major health care decision is made by government bureaucrats. We get what they say we will get for free . . . in return, they get to decide what health care procedures are vital. Same thing with food production. Government tells us what we can and cannot eat. Socialism has nothing to do with social equality. The richest people on earth are socialists!"

I told him, "You have a point. Socialist leaders live in walled-off communities. We live in squalor. They eat to their heart's content. We eat scraps from putrid piles of garbage. No one in a socialist society is supposed to be better off. They're certainly better off."

Paul agreed. "Indeed, they are."

I replied, "So, it's not about social equality?"

"Not at all."

I asked, "What's it about?"

He responded, "There's another book I want you to see. It's called *The Communist Manifesto*. Let me get it for you."

I recognized the book. They taught it at the GSB Academy. The curriculum there was heavily skewed toward the left, and the teachers were all socialists. I was on their side until Paul set me straight.

• • •

> The immediate aim of the Communists is the same as that of all the other proletariat parties: formation of the proletariat into a class, the overthrow of the bourgeois supremacy, conquest of political power by the proletariat[268]

He said, "There it is in black and white: they're interested in control, not economic prosperity. It's all about political power."

I said, "It's common ownership. Democratic workers controlling the means of production."

He laughed. "That's the fluffy version of Marxism. When was the last democratic election?" I didn't answer.

He said, "It was in 2036. Do you control the means of production?"

I said, "Of course not!" He asked me why. I didn't say anything again.

"Because socialism is in direct control of industries and social services. It demands absolute domination of the marketplace by an overpowering influential centralized government. The force of socialism is it is forced socially.[269] It's the economic system imposed by communism. It sounds wonderful—in the end, it's government manipulation."

"That's not what my teachers told me," I replied.

"They're wrong," he said. "See for yourself."

> . . . the theory of the Communists may be summed up in the single sentence: Abolition of private property[270]

I put the book down and looked at Paul. In his hand was a small piece of paper with a strange symbol on it. I said, "What's that?"

He answered, "It's a letter. Remember the email between Ikner and Bell? This document is related."

> I met with the others today in Santa Clara, and we decided it is time to reevaluate our plan . . . Farmers and ranchers all over the country are refusing to work—we cannot reallocate foodstuffs if they are not being produced in the first place . . . If we cannot control the food supply, we are going to have to find another way

to replace the old profit-based economy. The socialization strategy we started last year is in jeopardy right now. Here are the steps we need to take to get it back on track before the public revolts . . .

I told him, "This is a letter from Majority Leader Ikner to President Bell. Where did you get it?"

He said, "Remember the guard who brought in the books? He gave it to me."

. . . Keep the pressure on. Look for ways to increase insecurity. Never let the enemy score points. Cut off their support networks. Whatever you do, keep the people in the dark. We have not lost control yet . . .

"He keeps saying 'we,'" I remarked. I asked who the other people were. Paul grabbed the paper.

"These guys are the technocrats." He handed me the paper again. "See this symbol at the top of the letter?"

I asked, "The one with the pyramid?"

"That's the one," he affirmed. "It represents human development. The technocrats are the pyramid. They're a cabal."

"A cabal?" I repeated.

"There's a select group of people out there who are covertly running this country," he explained. "They meet twice every year in a discrete location. Their leader is a man named Dr. Nyell."

I said, "Dr. Clint Nyell. He's that super-rich techy guy from England."

"That's him," Paul said, confirming my recollection.

I told him, "This is crazy."

He pointed to the symbol and said, "See the emblem with two squiggly lines inside the pyramid. That's the Aquarius sign. It represents the next stage of human evolution. Aquarius is tied to organizations, humanitarian efforts, innovation, and group identity. It is seen as a force for breaking up old structures."

I responded, "What does that have to do with anything?"

"The technocrats," he said, "are preparing us for the next new age. Remember the email? According to them, we're entering a period of revolution fueled by technical invention. You see, Tim, Aquarius is linked with information and technology. This so-called new age is all about erecting a more egalitarian world. Another key aspect of this reputed technological age is humanitarianism without prejudice or preference—the group takes precedence over the individual."

I said, "Kinda like that article: '*The Rights Of Individuals Are Superseded By The Overall Good Of The State.*'"

"You got it!" he reacted. "It will come as no surprise for you to learn that the 'Harmony and Tolerance' idea is a New Age concept. New Age spirituality is about pluralism. It's a religious and a social movement."

It was then I realized the horrible mistake I had made. I thought I knew what socialism was. I was wrong. Socialism wasn't really about freeing workers from corporate slavery. It actually made people more subservient to corporations. It was an organized umbrella religion that benefitted the ruling class.

It finally hit me. The ultimate goal of the New Socialist Movement was neopagan hegemony!

· · ·

I asked Paul how many technocrats there were. He didn't have an exact answer. He told me, "Less than a thousand."

I responded, "That's not many people. How did they get into power?"

"The answer," he said, "is in the letter."

> . . . Deceive the American people. Tell them anything. Tell them we can enhance their lives . . .

"They lied to us. They told us capitalism was dead. Then they lied again. They said socialism was the only way out. Nothing could be further from the truth. Socialist economies impoverish people."

> . . . Hold out a false guarantee. Make them think they are going to get some relief. We must promise great things to stay in control . . .

"They promised a better life for all. The world was falling apart all around us. They offered hope. It was a trap. Their solution to the problem produced a worse net result than the problem itself."

> . . . Use isolation tactics to get them to stay with us . . .

"They regulated the flow of information, and they blocked access to non-socialist sources of information. Debate was stymied."

> . . . Eliminate all critics and voices against our agenda . . .

"They made their detractors radioactive. The media effectively labeled them racist or misogynistic. They did away with their competition."

. . . Make the American people depend on us . . .

"The economy was in horrible shape. They kept it in a malaise on purpose. We couldn't help ourselves. We had to rely on them."

. . . Take away their liberties. We cannot abolish private property unless we abolish freedom . . .

"Our rights were taken away one by one. Before we knew it, they were all gone."

• • •

"There you have it," Paul said. "These are shrewd individuals. They know how to manipulate the masses for their own purposes. They became our leaders by leading us in the wrong direction. They cut off the escape route so we couldn't flee. See, Tim, when the many rest on the backs of the few, the few become rulers.[271] Demagogues show up whenever economies slow down.[272] Despot leaders feed off desperate needers."[273]

Before I could say a word he went over to the secret chamber. "There's another article in here I want you to see." I asked him what it was about. He told me it had to do with cash.

I laughed. "Cash! We don't use cash anymore!"

"Cash was important," he said as he was shuffling through some papers. "It gave us privacy. Cash allowed us to remain anonymous during routine transactions. Besides, it was acceptable everywhere. It's more vital than you think. This article explains why."

Cash Is Not King Anymore

November 8, 2034 In a move to eliminate counterfeit bills, President Bell stunned the nation by announcing the discontinuation of millions of high-denomination currency notes . . . Bank notes worth fifty dollars and above will be invalid starting next year. On January 1, 2035, they will no longer be considered legal tender . . .

"The ban was heralded as a sweeping move against corruption. It was also touted as an anti-terrorism resolution. The idea behind the recall was simple. Crack down on tax evaders who keep all their assets in cash. Reduce the size of the black market economy. The change, however, caused upheaval across the land. Millions of people were forced to line up at the banks . . . they had to deposit the money and make their assets official or exchange their old bills for approved notes."

I noticed that he was holding a piece of paper. I asked, "Is that another newspaper clipping?"

He looked at me. "It's a memo from Earl Ikner. Want to see it?"

I responded, "Of course!"

> . . . The decision last November to remove and replace large-de-nomination paper money is being widely criticized . . . One unin-tended consequence has been a serious cash shortage. The move took too much cash out of circulation . . .

"The abrupt ban on large bills was poorly executed. It backfired on the poor," Paul maintained. I asked him how.

He said, "Wages vanished and millions of Americans lost their jobs. Millions more couldn't access their own money. All of a sudden tens of millions of people all over the country were left without the means to engage economically. It's in the memo."

> . . . Our attempt to enact order has not gone as planned. Many people do not have bank accounts. Credit card and digital wal-let use in the United States has been in decline since 2032. Large percentages of transactions are being done in cash . . . The digital infrastructure is in terrible shape all across the country. Mobile connections are particularly poor in the nation's rural areas. The push to go cashless has deepened the digital divide between urban and rural districts . . .

He said, "You're probably wondering why they did all this. There were beneficiaries."

I replied, "Like who?"

"Duralonics was the primary beneficiary," he alleged.

I said, "The company Bell founded?"

"Yes. Demonetization is very 'lucrative.' Sense Bell's announcement, Duralonics has been raking in money." He proceeded to pull out another piece of paper.

I asked, "What's that?"

He said, "It's a report from Duralonics."

> . . . Since demonetization was announced in 2034, use of the WICAN platform has soared . . . WICAN is the largest digital

commerce platform in the United States. Soon it will be all over the world . . .

"Demonetization was great for Duralonics. Because of it hundreds of millions of new users were pushed onto that company's digital network. WICAN is way ahead of any other e-commerce platform. It's hard to do business without it."

I said, "This is intriguing stuff, but what does any of this have to do with the Revolution?"

"Funny you should ask," he replied. "It just so happens that I have the answer right here."

Kentucky Congressman Zachary Stephenson Beats Incumbent Mark Duke Bell To Win US Presidency

Nobody thought he would win, but it looks like Zachary Stephenson is going to be the next president of the United States . . . "Last Tuesday's election was a major win for antisocialists," said the leader of the newly formed Originalist Party. "Zachary Stephenson rode a wave of anger against government corruption. The voters chose him as their new leader because they are sick and tired of cronyism." . . .

"It took a while," Paul said, "but the American people finally woke up. Bell paid a heavy political price for his war on cash. He was voted out of office."

I asked him again, "What does any of this have to do with the Revolution?" His response was kind of amazing.

"Originalist Zachary Stephenson's win on November 4, 2036 was unexpected. It was like Republican Abraham Lincoln's victory in 1860. There was a revolt. Lawsuits were filed immediately after the election!"

"Against whom?" I shouted.

He shook his head. "Against President-Elect Stephenson! See for yourself."

. . . Lawsuits are piling up against President-Elect Stephenson and the Originalist Party. One lawsuit that contends the Electoral College is unconstitutional has made it all the way to the Supreme Court . . .

"That's the way they did it for more than two centuries. The Electoral College was the formal body that elected the president. It was a compromise between having the president elected by Congress and having the president elected by the popular vote.

"See, Tim, Americans didn't elect their president directly. They voted for an elector. Each state had the same number of electors in the Electoral College as it had representatives and senators in the Congress. These electors met after the general election in their respective state capitals on the Monday following the second Wednesday in December. Their votes decided the next president."

I handed him the article. "I hate to beat a dead horse, but what does this have to do with the Revolution?" He didn't reply. He went over to the door instead.

I said, "Do you have an answer?" He kept staring at the door. I said again, "Do you have an answer for me?" He didn't say a word. I thought, *This is great. He stopped talking to me all of the sudden.* I said one last time, "Can you tell me anything?" He walked over to his bunk and looked down at the floor. I told him, "Well?"

"The rest is difficult," he responded.

I said, "Just tell me!"

"The New Socialists were upset because Bell won the popular vote but still lost the election. In their minds Stephenson's victory was illegitimate because more Americans had voted for Bell. The popular vote didn't matter," he said pointing to the article. "You needed 270 electoral votes to win the presidency. Bell got 266. He fell short."

I stopped him in mid-sentence. "Bell falling short . . . I never thought I'd hear anyone say that."

"You've heard it now," he remarked. "Bell lost the election. He ended up losing more electors than Stephenson."

I said, "That doesn't make any sense."

"What doesn't make any sense?" he asked.

"Why wasn't he President?"

Paul shook his head. "He was . . . for a short while. His presidency was over before it began."

I replied, "What's that supposed to mean?"

He said, "It's a long story." I told him we seem to have plenty of time, and then we both sat down.

• • •

"Here's where it gets disturbing. The Electoral College was challenged on the grounds that it 'gave small states too much control.' The Bell administration asked the Supreme Court to decide whether states had the authority to make their own laws."

I asked him, "Are there more documents?"

"As a matter of fact, there are," he answered. "If you'll give me a minute, I'll get them out for you."

I told him, "Take all the time you need."

While he was looking I went over to the door. I said, "Do you think we'll ever get out of here?" Paul's answer was that he didn't know. I asked him is it even possible to be free anymore. He said with God all things were possible, and then he made me sit. I went to my bunk immediately. I knew he had something important to show me because of the look in his eyes.

America's High Court Overturns 2036 Presidential Election

> In a unanimous decision, the Court held that the federal government had the power to establish a uniform rule for the entire nation . . . Writing for the Court, Chief Justice Catherine Friederike Dornburg said, "Laws must proceed from Washington . . . The electors' votes violate the Fourteenth Amendment's equal protection guarantee. States do not have the authority to set their own election rules.". . .

"So," he said, "you want to know about the overthrow?"

I asked, "What overthrow?"

He said, "The overthrow of 2037. It was the Supreme Court's fault. Mark Duke Bell got another shot at the presidency. The Supreme Court stole the election for the incumbent. See, Tim, the Electoral College was important. It gave voice to the nation's smaller states. If the president was selected by a national popular vote, large urban areas would've completely dominated. Small and rural states would've become irrelevant. The process helped hold America together for more than two hundred years. Its repeal brought about conflict that would lead to the Revolution."

He got up again. I said, "Where are you going this time?"

He looked at me. "Back into the chamber."

I said, "Aren't you gonna tell me what happened?"

"I will," he said, "if you just relax. There was a lot of turmoil. The decision inflamed regional differences. America was split in two. There was a wave of anti-government protests. Thousands of protesters flooded the streets. Five people were killed in protest-related violence. Bell, meanwhile, ordered the US armed forces onto the streets to maintain order."

I asked, "Is there something wrong with maintaining order?"

He said, "No. It's what he did next." I followed him to the other side of the cell.

"What did he do?"

He said, "I'll show you, if you let me go into my chamber."

• • •

It didn't take long for him to retrieve the newspaper articles. He handed me the first one.

Bell Plans To Rewrite US Constitution

Amid growing unrest and after weeks of violent protests, President Bell on Monday signed an executive order calling for an assembly to draft a new version of the country's Constitution. While he provided few details, he said that the new body, which will consist of fifty-five expert delegates, will have the authority to redefine the President's executive powers . . .

I asked, "What's an expert delegate?"

"Expert delegate is the same as saying technocrat," he answered.

I asked him, "Are they the pyramid?"

"They're the top of the pyramid," he explained. "Bell wanted them to rewrite America's Constitution."

I looked at him. "Why on earth would they rewrite the Constitution?"

He said, "Remember the letter from Majority Leader Ikner to President Bell?"

I said, "Yeah."

He said, "Do you remember what he wrote?"

I asked, "What did he write?"

"Ikner said to Bell, 'We anticipate there is going to be a rebellion—we need to be ready when it happens.' It was all part of the plan."

I cried out, "What plan!"

He looked over his shoulder. "The plan laid out in 2032. Think back to the email. 'We can establish a socialist majority.' This was their scheme all along. They sped up the collapse of the capitalist system by precipitating the crisis that led to the Revolution. The end of the republic didn't come as a shock. It was mapped out ahead of time. The socialists had allies. Look at this article."

Armed Forces Back President Bell

The United States military has declared its allegiance to the President, as the country faces a mounting political and constitutional crisis . . .

"The Revolution began on January 20, 2037, the same day the inauguration of Zachary Stephenson was supposed to have taken place. Tens of thousands of demonstrators demanding justice went to the nation's capital to protest the Bell administration's naked power grab. The demonstrators were met by socialist counter-protesters who were also in town.

"Things quickly spun out of control as protesters and counter-protesters faced off and clashed around the city. Marchers began to fight one another. They started beating each other with sticks, clubs, and makeshift weapons. The level of fighting in D.C. was far worse than anything I'd seen before. The violence left 241 people dead and thousands injured."

"Was that the end?" I asked.

He said, "That wasn't the end. The end came ten days later." I asked him so what happened. He handed me the last newspaper article. "This is what happened," he replied.

Supreme Court Strips Lawmakers Of Power

In an amazing move anti-socialists are calling a coup, the United States Supreme Court has stripped Congress of its constitutional duties . . . The court said it would take over all "legislative powers" until the political crisis is resolved . . .

"Army units were called out to quell the bloodshed the next day. January 21st marked the point of no return for the dictatorship. Our democratically elected government was forced to resign and a provisional government headed by the fifty-five expert delegates was established in its place. A couple of days later, on January 23rd, the provisional government issued the legendary Order X. Military commanders were told to obey only the orders of the fifty-five expert delegates and not those of the old government. Then, on January 30th, the Supreme Court blocked a motion that would've prevented the expert delegates from building a new government. The justices gave themselves the legislative controls that were once held by Congress. The ruling allowed the court to write laws itself. It also meant that the three branches of government would be controlled by the ruling New Socialist Party.

"The outcome of the 2036 presidential election was foreordained. The court was, of course, stacked with New Socialists. Bell packed the judiciary with his own supporters. Once the New Socialists had control of the government, they hijacked the country.

"The military dispatched army units to take over schools, factories, and government organizations. Religious and cultural symbols were destroyed in the process . . . they tried to eradicate the past.

"In addition to that, Bell called on young people 'to continue to rebel against the system.' These young people were formed into paramilitary groups called the Surge Alliance. They attacked anyone and anything they considered a threat to socialism. They went after religious leaders, as well as school teachers and journalists. Those with ties to the former government were particularly brutalized. Several thousand people died in the course of these persecutions.

"Once the New Socialists had gotten rid of the counterrevolutionaries, they began to enact social and political reforms. The provisional government came to power after the January Revolution. The old constitution was repealed on February 23rd . . . then the elites began to claim the land as their own. They drafted a new constitution. The new constitution, which acted as an informative propaganda document was ratified on July 10th, 2037. Finally, on August 2nd, they passed a law abolishing the office of president. Mark Duke Bell was declared absolute dictator. He's been the nation's shepherd ever since."

I said, "What happened to President-Elect Stephenson?" He looked away. I asked him the same question again.

"He's dead," Paul answered. "They killed him! Stephenson and his wife were gunned down!"

I said, "What! How do you know all this?"

"I was Chief of Staff for President-Elect Stephenson. I'm Paul Benjamin," he replied. "I'm in here because I was part of the Stephenson administration. President-Elect Stephenson staffed the White House with Christians. They said we were proselytizing. Government officials came to our headquarters and told us we had to get out. We were taken as prisoners of war."

I shouted, "You've been in here since 2037!"

He said, "Yes. I was totally alone until you got here. Apparently they're running out of space."

• • •

I started pacing. Paul said, "You seem confused."

I looked at him. "I am confused. You said, 'The end began at the beginning with an institution.' You also said, 'Slavery for one group of people produced slavery for all people.' The end came in 2037. I know how it happened. The government gained control over the people. There's still one thing that you haven't explained. What role did slavery play in the Revolution?"

"I already told you," he said. "'Slavery started a chain of events that caused America to go full circle.' Slavery was divisive. The Republican Party was formed in response to slavery. Abraham Lincoln was the first president from the Republican Party. His election caused the Southern States to secede. There was a civil war. After the war was over Republicans had absolute control over the South for the next twelve years. And for six and a half decades they dominated the presidency and control of Congress.

"Republicans left the market alone. The 1920's saw a return to a laissez-faire market economy. The stock market ballooned due to margin purchases. Overspeculation led to incorrectly high stock prices. The Roaring '20s came to a screeching halt when the US stock market took a historic dive. The 1929 stock market crash signaled the beginning of the *Great Depression*. The *Great Depression* was the worst economic crisis in American history. Many blamed President Hoover for the country's economic woes. They elected Franklin D. Roosevelt president in 1932 because they believed he could fight the *Great Depression*. Roosevelt pledged a new deal for the American people. The US government grew significantly under President Roosevelt.

"Life was easier after the *New Deal*. Still, getting ahead was difficult for some people. Blacks didn't have the same opportunities whites had. President Lyndon Johnson introduced his own vision for America in 1964. He called his vision the *Great Society*. The *Great Society* had unintended consequences. American culture had polarized into two completely different ideological camps. Americans became divided along party lines. There was a new culture war. Republicans and Democrats had different standards. They couldn't agree on anything. However, there was one thing they could agree on: control.

"Government grew again under Presidents Bush and Obama. They fundamentally transformed America. The housing market became a casino. Overspeculation drove up home prices. The market tanked after the housing bubble burst. Wall Street began to disintegrate. The economy went into steep decline at the end of 2008. Government policies made the situation even worse. The nation never fully recovered.

"The federal government owed too much money. Officials at the Treasury Department found themselves in a position where they couldn't repay the principal and interest on the national debt. They decided they were better off not paying it at all. The United States went into default. That caused the economic system to collapse.

"Most voters felt President Matsin was to blame. Mark Duke Bell was elected Commander in Chief in November 2032. He was the president for a new generation. Things got worse. The New Socialists rigged the system in their favor. They made us rely on them. President Bell tried to eliminate cash. The push to go cashless deepened the digital divide between urban and rural districts. Bell paid a heavy political price for his war on cash. He was voted out of office.

"Bell didn't accept the election results. He asked the Supreme Court to intervene. The Court overturned President-Elect Stephenson's victory. Tens of thousands of pro-Stephenson demonstrators went to Washington to protest the administration's naked power grab. Army units were called out to quell the violence. The end came in 2037. America's Supreme Court took over legislative powers. The old government was forced to resign and a new government was established in its place. The New Socialists gained control over the people. Here we are 261 years later . . . we're all slaves now."

• • •

The answer I got was unexpected. Everything came together in 2037. The end did begin at the beginning with an institution. Slavery led to communism, and communism led to slavery. It was a confluence of events.

Paul said, "There's one last thing . . . the time of my departure is at hand. I'm the only one left. Everyone else from the Stephenson administration is gone. They're getting rid of the loose ends, including me. I'm scheduled for execution." I asked him why he didn't tell me and then I began to weep bitterly.

He said, "It wasn't necessary. We have little time left. Tell people the truth. I'm not going to be here for much longer. It's up to you to get the word out. Do you remember everything?"

Without skipping a beat I replied, "Absolutely. I have an eidetic memory."

He said, "From the moment I saw you, I knew you were special. You're here for a reason. God has given you a gift. Use your photographic memory to tell others what I told you. Find Silas Maccabee. He's another inmate. Go to him. There are still things we can do."

I grabbed his shoulders. "What are we supposed to do? We have no weapons. Guns are illegal. The economy is rigged in favor of certain groups. A few corporations own everything. The *Invisible Hand* was lopped off! Besides, technology has backed us into a corner. We can't do anything unless we're approved. Every move we make is monitored by the network. The whole world is electronic. How are we supposed to fight back if we can't even buy or sell?"

"Those are all good points," he affirmed.

I went to the other side of the cell to cry. Paul waited for me to regain my composure. I looked up at him from the floor and said, "There isn't any hope! These parasites took everything from us. The New Socialists control every single aspect of our life! Grandma was right . . . they're a bunch of thieves. All is lost."

He said, "You're wrong. There is hope. Our hope is in a man."

I replied, "Man? What man?"

He told me, "The Son of man."

I said, "What are you talking about?"

"Emmanuel. See, Tim, to speak to man, God became a man. He lowered Himself to our level because we cannot raise ourselves to His. It all began two thousand years ago in the land of Israel. A virgin conceived and brought forth a Son. They called Him Emmanuel. The child grew and became strong in spirit, and the grace of God was upon Him. When He was thirty He began His ministry. He went about doing good and healing all who were oppressed by the devil, for God was with Him. He was a threat to the establishment. The leaders went out and plotted against Him. They led Him away to the high priest, and then they delivered Him to the governor. The men who held Him mocked Him and beat Him."

I thought, *Could this be the man in the dream?* I kept listening.

"The governor asked Him, 'Are You the King of the Jews' (Matthew 27:11 *NKJV*). The man answered, 'You say rightly that I am a king. For this cause I was born, and for this cause I have come into the world, that I should bear witness to the truth. Everyone who is of the truth hears My voice' (John 18:37 *NKJV*). The governor wanted to chastise Him and let Him go, but the crowd was insistent. He asked the people, 'Why, what evil has He done?' They cried out, 'Let Him be crucified' (Matthew 27:23 *NKJV*). So the governor, wanting to gratify the crowd, released a notorious prisoner to them; and he delivered the man, after he had scourged Him, to be crucified."

I shouted, "Who is He!"

He answered, "Jesus of Nazareth, the Christ. His coming was prophesied in the Old Testament. The LORD anointed Him to preach the Gospel to the poor. He sent Him to heal the brokenhearted, to proclaim liberty to the captives, to recover sight to the blind, and to set at liberty those who are oppressed."

• • •

It was at that moment, I knew, there was more to life than what I had been taught. The dreams were a premonition. Things started to change pretty quickly from there. God began a work in my heart. I saw the world around me from an entirely new perspective. It was like I was a different man.

A few hours later Paul was gone. The guards whisked him off to another room. Even though our conversations were over, I knew that my new life in Jesus Christ had just begun. It was still cold and dark inside my prison cell—yet, something wasn't the same. I saw a light shining in the darkness. For the first time in my life I had something to live for.

Endnotes

1. Ridolfi, Useful Maxims, 153.
2. Ridolfi, Useful Maxims, 82.
3. U.S. Const. Article IV, Section 4.
4. Daniel, Chronicle of America, 201.
5. U.S. Const. Article I, Section 1.
6. U.S. Const. Article I, Section 2.
7. U.S. Const. Article I, Section 3.
8. U.S. Const. Amendment XVII.
9. U.S. Const. Article V.
10. U.S. Const. Article II, Section 1.
11. U.S. Const. Article III, Section 1.
12. Ridolfi, Useful Maxims, 157.
13. Ridolfi, Useful Maxims, 157.
14. Daniel, Chronicle of America, 198.
15. Declaration of Independence, July 4, 1776.
16. Ridolfi, Useful Maxims, 149.
17. Ridolfi, Useful Maxims, 149.
18. Daniel, Chronicle of America, 22.
19. Daniel, Chronicle of America, 51.
20. Daniel, Chronicle of America, 65.
21. Daniel, Chronicle of America, 70.
22. Ridolfi, Useful Maxims, 96.
23. Ridolfi, Useful Maxims, 96.
24. Ridolfi, Useful Maxims, 96.
25. Ridolfi, Useful Maxims, 126.
26. Ridolfi, Useful Maxims, 126.
27. Ridolfi, Useful Maxims, 126.
28. Ridolfi, Useful Maxims, 117.
29. Ridolfi, Useful Maxims, 115.
30. Daniel, Chronicle of America, 133.
31. Daniel, Chronicle of America, 140.
32. Daniel, Chronicle of America, 150.
33. Daniel, Chronicle of America, 193.
34. Daniel, Chronicle of America, 238.
35. Daniel, Chronicle of America, 238.

36. Daniel, Chronicle of America, 240.
37. Daniel, Chronicle of America, 298.
38. Ridolfi, Useful Maxims, 108.
39. Ridolfi, Useful Maxims, 108.
40. Ridolfi, Useful Maxims, 108.
41. Ridolfi, Useful Maxims, 107.
42. Ridolfi, Useful Maxims, 107.
43. Ridolfi, Useful Maxims, 107.
44. Ridolfi, Useful Maxims, 148.
45. Thomas Jefferson to a committee of the Danbury Baptist association in the state of Connecticut, January 1, 1802.
46. U.S. Const. Amendment I.
47. Ridolfi, Useful Maxims, 109.
48. Darwin, On the Origin of Species, 280.
49. Xu, You, and Han, "An Archaeopteryx-like theropod from China and the origin of Avialae.", 465.
50. Ridolfi, Useful Maxims, 112.
51. Ridolfi, Useful Maxims, 112.
52. Ridolfi, Useful Maxims, 112.
53. Austin, "Excess Argon within Mineral Concentrates..."
54. Lewontin, "Billions and Billions of Demons.", 31.
55. Wilson, From So Simple A Beginning…, 882.
56. Wilson, From So Simple A Beginning…, 1238.
57. Callaway, "Genetic Adam and Eve did not live too far apart in time.", Paragraph 1.
58. Ham and Hodge, How Do We Know The Bible Is True? Volume 2, 237.
59. Wilson, From So Simple A Beginning…, 891.
60. Hitler, Mein Kampf, Volume 1, Chapter 11: Nation and Race.
61. Hitler, Mein Kampf, Volume 1, Chapter 11: Nation and Race.
62. U.S. Const. Amendment XIII, Section 1.
63. Daniel, Chronicle of America, 347.
64. Daniel, Chronicle of America, 350.
65. Daniel, Chronicle of America, 358.
66. Daniel, Chronicle of America, 363.
67. Daniel, Chronicle of America, 364.
68. Ridolfi, Useful Maxims, 62.
69. Ridolfi, Useful Maxims, 64.
70. Ridolfi, Useful Maxims, 66.
71. Daniel, Chronicle of America, 365.
72. Daniel, Chronicle of America, 375.
73. Daniel, Chronicle of America, 377.
74. Daniel, Chronicle of America, 391.
75. Daniel, Chronicle of America, 392.
76. Basler, Collected Works of Abraham Lincoln, 332-33.
77. Daniel, Chronicle of America, 397.
78. Daniel, Chronicle of America, 615.
79. Daniel, Chronicle of America, 623.
80. Fuess, Calvin Coolidge: The Man from Vermont, 500.
81. Daniel, Chronicle of America, 626.

82. Daniel, Chronicle of America, 645.
83. Ridolfi, Useful Maxims, 134.
84. Ridolfi, Useful Maxims, 135.
85. Smith, The Wealth of Nations, 572.
86. Ridolfi, Useful Maxims, 142.
87. Ridolfi, Useful Maxims, 134.
88. Ridolfi, Useful Maxims, 127.
89. Ridolfi, Useful Maxims, 136.
90. Ridolfi, Useful Maxims, 136.
91. Ridolfi, Useful Maxims, 139.
92. Ridolfi, Useful Maxims, 126.
93. Ridolfi, Useful Maxims, 126.
94. Ridolfi, Useful Maxims, 128.
95. Ridolfi, Useful Maxims, 126.
96. Daniel, Chronicle of America, 657.
97. President Franklin D. Roosevelt's first inaugural address, March 4, 1933.
98. President Franklin D. Roosevelt's first inaugural address, March 4, 1933.
99. Daniel, Chronicle of America, 659.
100. Daniel, Chronicle of America, 659.
101. Daniel, Chronicle of America, 659.
102. Daniel, Chronicle of America, 668.
103. Ridolfi, Useful Maxims, 57.
104. Ridolfi, Useful Maxims, 153.
105. Ridolfi, Useful Maxims, 153.
106. Ridolfi, Useful Maxims, 153.
107. Daniel, Chronicle of America, 738.
108. Ridolfi, Useful Maxims, 138.
109. Daniel, Chronicle of America, 513.
110. Daniel, Chronicle of America, 770.
111. Daniel, Chronicle of America, 772.
112. Daniel, Chronicle of America, 634.
113. Daniel, Chronicle of America, 788.
114. Daniel, Chronicle of America, 752.
115. Daniel, Chronicle of America, 791.
116. Ridolfi, Useful Maxims, 91.
117. Engel v. Vitale, 370 U.S. 421, 1962.
118. Abington School District v. Schempp, 374 U.S. 203, 1963.
119. Ridolfi, Useful Maxims, 94.
120. Daniel, Chronicle of America, 783.
121. Daniel, Chronicle of America, 803.
122. Daniel, Chronicle of America, 812.
123. Daniel, Chronicle of America, 815.
124. Ridolfi, Useful Maxims, 66.
125. Ridolfi, Useful Maxims, 66.
126. Ridolfi, Useful Maxims, 63.
127. President Lyndon Johnson's annual State of the Union Address to the Congress, January 8, 1964.
128. Daniel, Chronicle of America, 806.

129. Series of political speeches Woodrow Wilson made during the 1912 presidential campaign.
130. President Lyndon Johnson's address before Congress, November 27, 1963.
131. Ridolfi, Useful Maxims, 155.
132. Ridolfi, Useful Maxims, 58.
133. DeNavas-Walt and Proctor, "Income and Poverty in the United States: 2013.", Page 12, Figure 4.
134. Heritage Foundation research, 2012, http://www.familyfacts.org/charts/310/since-the-war-on-poverty-began-in-1964-welfare-spending-has-skyrocketed.
135. Rector, "Marriage: America's Greatest Weapon Against Child Poverty.", Chart 3.
136. Rector, "Marriage: America's Greatest Weapon Against Child Poverty.", Chart 11.
137. Rector, "Marriage: America's Greatest Weapon Against Child Poverty.", Chart 8.
138. Ridolfi, Useful Maxims, 153.
139. Ridolfi, Useful Maxims, 153.
140. Ridolfi, Useful Maxims, 154.
141. Ridolfi, Useful Maxims, 154.
142. Ridolfi, Useful Maxims, 154.
143. Ridolfi, Useful Maxims, 57.
144. Ridolfi, Useful Maxims, 57.
145. Daniel, Chronicle of America, 787.
146. Ridolfi, Useful Maxims, 74.
147. Ridolfi, Useful Maxims, 74.
148. Ridolfi, Useful Maxims, 74.
149. Ridolfi, Useful Maxims, 75.
150. Ridolfi, Useful Maxims, 75.
151. Ridolfi, Useful Maxims, 75.
152. Ridolfi, Useful Maxims, 73.
153. Ridolfi, Useful Maxims, 58.
154. Ridolfi, Useful Maxims, 58.
155. Sanger, "Suppression.", Paragraph 2.
156. Ridolfi, Useful Maxims, 147.
157. Ellis, Abrams, and Abrams, Personality Theories, 393.
158. Jane Roe et al. v. Henry Wade, District Attorney of Dallas County, decided by the US Supreme Court on January 22, 1973.
159. Sanger, "Birth Control Advances: A Reply to the Pope.", Birth Control Does Not Mean Abortion.
160. Pazol, Creanga, Burley, and Jamieson, "Abortion Surveillance - United States, 2011.", Table 13.
161. Death With Dignity Act, ORS 127.800-995, November 8, 1994.
162. Ridolfi, Useful Maxims, 143.
163. Ridolfi, Useful Maxims, 29.
164. Daniel, Chronicle of America, 816.
165. Daniel, Chronicle of America, 802.
166. Daniel, Chronicle of America, 802.
167. http://www.gallup.com/poll/166613/four-report-attending-church-last-week.aspx.
168. www.disastercenter.com/crime/uscrime.htm.
169. Ridolfi, Useful Maxims, 156.

170. Ridolfi, Useful Maxims, 93.
171. Ridolfi, Useful Maxims, 93.
172. Ridolfi, Useful Maxims, 81.
173. Ridolfi, Useful Maxims, 81.
174. Daniel, Chronicle of America, 827.
175. Ridolfi, Useful Maxims, 158.
176. Daniel, Chronicle of America, 822.
177. Ridolfi, Useful Maxims, 87.
178. Ridolfi, Useful Maxims, 46.
179. https://www.goodreads.com/work/quotes/824093-prometheus-rising.
180. Ridolfi, Useful Maxims, 88.
181. Ridolfi, Useful Maxims, 88.
182. Ridolfi, Useful Maxims, 87.
183. Ridolfi, Useful Maxims, 89.
184. Ridolfi, Useful Maxims, 87.
185. Ridolfi, Useful Maxims, 45.
186. Ridolfi, Useful Maxims, 52.
187. Ridolfi, Useful Maxims, 52.
188. Ridolfi, Useful Maxims, 52.
189. Ridolfi, Useful Maxims, 52.
190. Daniel, Chronicle of America, 835.
191. President Richard Nixon's address to the nation on the war in Vietnam, November 3, 1969.
192. President Ronald Reagan's first inauguration, January 20, 1981.
193. Daniel, Chronicle of America, 868.
194. Daniel, Chronicle of America, 927.
195. Milbank, "President Asks for Expanded Patriot Act.", Paragraph 3.
196. https://www.eff.org/nsa-spying/how-it-works.
197. United States District Court, Eastern District of Michigan Southern Division, Case No. 06-CV-10204, Honorable Anna Diggs Taylor.
198. 107th Congress Public Law 107-243, AUTHORIZATION FOR USE OF MILITARY FORCE AGAINST IRAQ RESOLUTION OF 2002, October 16, 2002.
199. President George W. Bush's address to the United Nations, September 12, 2002.
200. US Secretary of State's address to the United Nations Security Council, February 5, 2003.
201. Newport, "Seventy-Two Percent of Americans Support War Against Iraq."
202. Jones, "Rally Boosting Bush Approval Ratings."
203. http://www.cnn.com/2004/US/03/21/iraq.weapons/.
204. President George W. Bush's remarks on signing the American Dream Downpayment Act, December 16, 2003.
205. Public Law 95-128, 91 Stat. 1147, title VIII of the Housing and Community Development Act of 1977, 12 U.S.C. § 2901 et seq., October 12, 1977.
206. Public Law 110-343, 122 Stat. 3765, October 3, 2008.
207. Boswell, "TARP Did Not Save Us From A Great Depression, It Nearly Created One."
208. Samuelson, "Why TARP Has Been A Success Story."
209. Public Law 111-5, 123 Stat. 115, February 17, 2009.
210. Spectrum Group, "Trends in US High-Net-Worth Households 1997-2014."

211. http://www.factcheck.org/2014/10/obamas-numbers-october-2014-update/.

212. http://www.factcheck.org/2015/10/obamas-numbers-october-2015-update/.

213. DeNavas-Walt and Proctor, "Income and Poverty in the United States: 2014", Page 5, Figure 1.

214. DeNavas-Walt and Proctor, "Income and Poverty in the United States: 2014", Page 12, Figure 4.

215. President Barack Hussein Obama's second inaugural address, January 21, 2013.

216. Agreement Between the United States of America and the Republic of Iraq On the Withdrawal of United States Forces from Iraq and the Organization of Their Activities during Their Temporary Presence in Iraq, ratified by the Iraqi Parliament on November 27, 2008 approved by Iraq's presidential council on December 4, 2008.

217. http://thehill.com/policy/defense/260252-obama-it-would-be-a-mistake-to-use-ground-troops-against-isis.

218. Senator Barack Obama's campaign rally at the University of Missouri in Columbia, October 30, 2008.

219. Speaker of the House Nancy Pelosi's remarks at the 2010 Legislative Conference for the National Association of Counties, March 9, 2010.

220. Remarks made by Massachusetts Institute of Technology Economics professor Jonathan Gruber at the University of Pennsylvania during the Annual Health Economics Conference, October, 2013.

221. Ridolfi, Useful Maxims, 146.

222. Ridolfi, Useful Maxims, 146.

223. Ridolfi, Useful Maxims, 146.

224. National Federation of Independent Business v. Kathleen Sebelius, Secretary of Health and Human Services, 567 U.S., 2012.

225. U.S. Const. Article I, Section 8.

226. Majority Opinion, National Federation of Independent Business v. Sebelius, written by Chief Justice John Roberts, decided June 28, 2012.

227. David King v. Sylvia Mathews Burwell, Secretary of Health and Human Services, 576 U.S., 2015.

228. Public Law 79–404, 60 Stat. 237, June 11, 1946.

229. U.S. Const. Article I, Section 8.

230. U.S. Const. Article I, Section 8.

231. U.S. Const. Article III, Section 1.

232. U.S. Const. Article III, Section 2.

233. Dred Scott v. John F.A. Sandford, 60 U.S. 393, 1857.

234. U.S. Const. Article IV, Section 2.

235. U.S. Const. Article III, Section 2.

236. U.S. Const. Article I, Section 2.

237. Foner, Life and Writings of Douglas vol. 2, 472.

238. Carrie Buck v. John Hendren Bell, 274 U.S. 200, 1927.

239. Estelle T. Griswold and C. Lee Buxton v. Connecticut, 381 U.S. 479, 1965.

240. [S B 281] Approved March 20, 1924.

241. Fred Korematsu v. United States, 323 U.S. 214, 1944.

242. Lakhdar Boumediene, et al., Petitioners v. George W. Bush, President of the United States, et al., 553 U.S. 723, 2008.

243. Ridolfi, Useful Maxims, 148.

244. Ridolfi, Useful Maxims, 148.
245. Ridolfi, Useful Maxims, 151.
246. Ridolfi, Useful Maxims, 149.
247. Ridolfi, Useful Maxims, 149.
248. Ridolfi, Useful Maxims, 151.
249. Ridolfi, Useful Maxims, 149.
250. http://www.merriam-webster.com/dictionary/politically correct.
251. James Obergefell, et al., v. Richard Hodges, Director of the Ohio Department of Health, et al., 576 U.S., 2015.
252. Ridolfi, Useful Maxims, 154.
253. Ridolfi, Useful Maxims, 155.
254. Ridolfi, Useful Maxims, 155.
255. Ridolfi, Useful Maxims, 155.
256. https://www.goodreads.com/author/quotes/5451872.Alexander_Fraser_Tytler.
257. Webster's Ninth New Collegiate Dictionary, 1241.
258. Ridolfi, Useful Maxims, 66.
259. Ridolfi, Useful Maxims, 66.
260. Popper, The Open Society and Its Enemies Volume 1, 581.
261. Ridolfi, Useful Maxims, 67.
262. Popper, The Open Society and Its Enemies Volume 1, 581.
263. Ridolfi, Useful Maxims, 99.
264. Ridolfi, Useful Maxims, 99.
265. Ridolfi, Useful Maxims, 99.
266. https://www.brainyquote.com/quotes/authors/v/vladimir_lenin.html.
267. Ridolfi, Useful Maxims, 132.
268. Marx and Engels, The Communist Manifesto, 33.
269. Ridolfi, Useful Maxims, 142.
270. Marx and Engels, The Communist Manifesto, 34.
271. Ridolfi, Useful Maxims, 153.
272. Ridolfi, Useful Maxims, 134.
273. Ridolfi, Useful Maxims, 156.

Bibliography

Austin, S. A. "Excess Argon within Mineral Concentrates from the New Dacite Lava Dome at Mount St. Helens Volcano." *Creation Ex Nihilo Technical Journal* 10.3 (1996) 335–43.

Basler, Roy P., ed. *Collected Works of Abraham Lincoln Volume VIII.* Rutgers University Press, 1953.

Boswell, Jim. "TARP Did Not Save Us From A Great Depression, It Nearly Created One." *Businessinsider*, October 5, 2010. https://www.businessinsider.com/tarp-great-depression-2010–10.

Callaway, Ewen. "Genetic Adam and Eve Did Not Live Too Far Apart in Time." *Nature Journal*, August 6, 2013. doi:10.1038/nature.2013.13478.

Daniel, Clifton. *Chronicle of America.* DK Publishing, 1997.

Darwin, Charles. *On the Origin of Species by Means of Natural Selection, or the Preservation of Favoured Races in the Struggle for Life* (November 24, 1859).

DeNavas-Walt, Carmen and Bernadette D. Proctor. "Income and Poverty in the United States: 2013." *United States Census Bureau Current Population Report Number P60–249* (September 16, 2014).

———. "Income and Poverty in the United States: 2014." *United States Census Bureau Current Population Report Number P60–252* (September 2015).

Ellis, Albert, et al. *Personality Theories: Critical Perspectives.* Sage., 2009.

Foner, Philip S. *Life and Writings of Douglas vol. 2.* International, 1976.

Fuess, Claude M. *Calvin Coolidge: The Man from Vermont* (first published 1940).

Ham, Ken, and Hodge Bodie. *How Do We Know The Bible Is True? Volume 2.* Master Books, August 2012.

Hitler, Adolf. *Mein Kampf.* July 18, 1925.

Jones, Jeffrey M. "Rally Boosting Bush Approval Ratings." *gallup.com*, April 3, 2003. https://news.gallup.com/poll/8119/rally-boosting-bush-approval-ratings.aspx.

Lewontin, Richard. "Billions and Billions of Demons." *The New York Review* (January 9, 1997).

Marx Karl and Engels Friedrich. *The Communist Manifesto* (Published in London in 1848).

Milbank, Dana. "President Asks for Expanded Patriot Act." *Washington Post*, September 11, 2003. https://www.washingtonpost.com/archive/politics/2003/09/11/president-asks-for-expanded-patriot-act/5fb97ba3-ab6a-423c-b6da-047316ef4cf1/.

Bibliography

Newport, Frank. "Seventy-Two Percent of Americans Support War Against Iraq." *Gallup*, March 24, 2003. https://news.gallup.com/poll/8038/seventytwo-percent-americans-support-war-against-iraq.aspx.

Pazol, Karen, et al. "Abortion Surveillance—United States, 2011." *Morbidity and Mortality Weekly Report (MMWR)* 63(SS11) (November 28, 2014) 1–41.

Popper, Karl Raimund. *The Open Society and Its Enemies Volume 1*. Routledge, 1945.

Rector, Robert. "Marriage: America's Greatest Weapon Against Child Poverty." *Heritage*, September 16, 2010. https://www.heritage.org/poverty-and-inequality/report/marriage-americas-greatest-weapon-against-child-poverty-0.

Ridolfi, Brian. *Useful Maxims: In a World of Empty Speak*. Ambassador International, 2012.

Samuelson, Robert J. "Why TARP Has Been A Success Story." *Washington Post*, March 27, 2011. https://www.washingtonpost.com/opinions/why-tarp-has-been-a-success-story/2011/03/25/AFEe6jkB_story.html.

Sanger, Margaret. "Birth Control Advances: A Reply to the Pope." Source: Margaret Sanger Papers, Sophia Smith Collection, Smith College (1931).

———. "Suppression." *The Woman Rebel* 1.4 (June 25, 1914).

Smith, Adam. *The Wealth of Nations* (W. Strahan and T. Cadell, London, 1776). This edition is based on the fifth edition as edited and annotated by Edwin Cannan in 1904 (Bantam Classics; Annotated edition, March 4, 2003).

Spectrum Group. "Trends in US High-Net-Worth Households 1997–2014." *Marketing Charts*. https://www.marketingcharts.com/demographics-and-audiences/household-income-52487/attachment/spectremgroup-high-net-worth-households-1997–2014-mar2015.

Webster's Ninth New Collegiate Dictionary (Merriam-Webster Inc., 1985).

Wilson, Edward O. *From So Simple A Beginning, The Four Great Books Of Charles Darwin*. Norton, 2006.

Xu, X., et al. "An Archaeopteryx-like Theropod from China and the Origin of Avialae." *Nature.com*, July 27, 2011. https://www.nature.com/articles/nature10288.

www.ingramcontent.com/pod-product-compliance
Lightning Source LLC
Chambersburg PA
CBHW051527050726
47503CB00014B/2054